The Tale of the

Terrali

Nighthunters

Rebecca Hart-Lyon

Published by Rebecca Hart-Lyon

ISBN: 978-0-6151-8261-2

This story is dedicated to my family and friends who convinced me that I can actually tell a story, and have waited nearly five years for me to tell it.

And it is also dedicated to nearly every acquaintance that I've made in my journey through life that has inspired some part of this story.

Prologue: Budora, the Jewel

It was arguable whether the classroom or the teacher was more ancient. Wittig fidgeted in the old wooden chair in the first row and adjusted his tight knit cap over his ears. He let his gaze wander around the old schoolroom, an adjunct to the Great Temple of Va'Lator. For two millennia students of theology had sat in this very room, in this very seat, listening to this very lecture and he was sure that they could not have been any more ready and eager than he. He had been studying Valazen theology since he could read and was in no hurry to finish his seminary and become Ven. He enjoyed studying, learning, debating, interpreting. While ascending to priesthood was the ultimate honor of all Valazen theologists, he simply wanted to know everything. He fidgeted again and took in a huge breath of the air in the schoolroom through his tiny nose. He closed his eyes and marveled at the multitude of priests that had sat in his same wooden chair and breathed that very same air as he had. He looked around at the other men and women as they arrived in the schoolroom. He was the youngest, though he looked much older.

He looked completely Elven, except for his ears which he kept covered by a hat. For his entire life he was regarded as pure Elven and lived as an Elf in the largest city in the Elven City-States, Tesvo-nar, with his Elven mother. No Elf suspected his tainted blood.

"Wittig!"

The anxious whisper came from behind him. Wittig turned around to see his classmate Ubjean walking briskly up the aisle towards him so

1

he pulled his books from the chair beside him to clear the seat he had been holding for him.

"Wittig, dear boy, how early did you get here to get that seat?"

Wittig pulled his hat down over his ears awkwardly and frowned back at Ubjean.

"Since right after morning prayers, of course!"

"Good Va'Haluc! You know the Book of Illust Creation better than Gweutan-ven himself!"

Ubjean knew better than anyone how passionately Wittig embraced the Valazen. He primarily studied Va'Haluc, and knew every tale, every myth, every prayer ever given to the god of Darkness, Night and Dreams.

"I hope you don't plan to question poor Gweutan-ven until nightfall!"

"Why of course I do!"

Wittig grinned widely back at Ubjean. He adored being known for his obsessive devoutness.

"Besides, he's reading his translation of the Emperor Jayess version today! Imagine that, Ubjean, the Emperor Jayess version, read in Elven! To us!"

Ubjean rolled his eyes and brushed the sight of Wittig's silly smiling face away. Wittig was right though. Never before in Elven history had the Emperor Jayess version been translated and discussed. The schoolroom was packed with Ven and theologists, Wittig being the first of them to arrive in the schoolroom. His excitement was not unrivaled, however, as this was truly a monumental reading.

It was only in the past two centuries that Elves and Humans had resumed diplomatic ties and commercial relations. There had been nearly four millennia of cold hard years between the two races. It was Emperor Ramerko who had finally come on horseback 213 years ago. His high court carried no weapons upon entering the Elven City-State of Hammeli-nar. He delivered the Emperor Jayess version of the Book of Illust Creation to the High Priestess Karoutes-ven. She had gracefully greeted Ramerko on that day as the Dwarves had been running correspondence between her and Ramerko for years, and this was to be the culmination of the peace treaty, the humans returning the Book of Illust Creation.

Tales of the beginning of the isolation between Elves and Men vary greatly. Thousands of years ago, the races lived among each other as one nation. A holy war began. It was a war between interpretations of the Valazen history. Humans had become more passionate and faithful than the intellectual, logical, critical elves. The Book of Illust Creation, so unique that the only copy believed to exist disappeared sometime in 3235 from the Temple of Va'Lator. Humans and Elves were quick to blame each other for the disappearance and war ensued resulting in four thousand years of isolation.

Neither Human nor Elven history had the missing scroll turned up, and both races rewrote the legends for themselves. The Emperor Jayess version of the Great Book of Creation was written in 3945, over 3000 years ago, and has been the version studied and prayed since.

The Elven version changed nearly every century. As time passed and the Elves became more and more critical and discerning, the versions were edited and refined to make the sense of the day.

To reconcile the races meant reconciling the two versions of the Book of Illust Creation. Finally, in 7012, the two races began communicating between each other through the Dwarves and it was agreed and conferred that the reconciliation would begin. Emperor Ramerko agreed to bring the Emperor Jayess version of the Book of Illust Creation to the Elves in 7030.

Ramerko choreographed his arrival perfectly with his entire high court. He dismounted his party at the arch of Karoutes-ven's gardens and marched forward with his court in their ceremonial dress. He addressed her with direct eye contact. They all kneeled in perfect unison before her throne and he placed the aged leather bound Illust Creation at her feet. Karoutes-ven's hardened face, it is said, softened as she stood and picked up the book. She then placed a Ven kiss on Ramerko's forehead. And thus was the end of the millennia of cold between the Elves and Humans.

Relations began again quickly, and Humans traveled to the Elven City-States by the hundreds. The Elves were welcoming, but still regarded Humans as less intelligent and less worthy of the Valazen favor.

Wittig nudged Ubjean as the old Gweutan-ven approached the ancient lectern. The old Ven adjusted his spectacles and opened the enormous leather-bound book. He took another inhalation of the ancient holy air and held his breath to listen. Gweutan-ven began his reading to the silent Elven audience.

"The Great Jewel

"The Eminent Mother fashioned the skies for herself and was content. She delivered to herself two sons, Coveal and Mindal, light and darkness. She then felt pride and fulfillment. She adored her sons and her universe and wished to bestow them a gift, and thus created the world of Budora the Great Jewel of the Universe.

"The Eminent Mother bestowed upon the Great Jewel four magical immortal races known as the Prieran Beasts to tend to Budora. There were the woodlike crawlers called Rodal who scratched over the face of the rock and polished it to a constant sparkle. The Gemal tunneled beneath the face of Budora, and crushed and churned the jewel into countless perfectly cut gems. The giant wet, rolling Flotal who squirmed and rolled like worms over the rock, kept it shining and clean. And the beautiful Atmal, the giant winged beasts that flew above Budora and could reach its highest faceted peaks.

"The Great Beasts had no minds, no will or intention. For many hundreds of millennia they existed in this fashion. The two sons also adored the Budora, and while Mindal shone his light upon the Great Jewel and caused it to sparkle, Coveal admired its beauty in the darkness.

"The Burning Jewel

"The two sons cherished the Great Jewel of Budora. Dark Coveal sought Budora for himself and wished to live and amuse himself in the paradise with the other Great Beasts, but being ethereal was unable to take solid form in the world. Mindal on the other hand cherished Budora from afar and felt it was most beautiful in the light when left to shine on its own. Coveal spent millennia surrounding Budora with his inky darkness but would be cast away into the skies by Mindal. These conflicts between light and darkness were the birth of night and day.

The Tale of the Terrali Nighthunters

"In an effort to end the contest of Light and Darkness, the Eminent Mother then created the Valazen, a tiny immortal race who lived amongst the beasts and collected the cut jewels and treasures from the great beasts for the Eminent Mother and her sons to adorn themselves as the noble gods they were. They followed the Gemal through the rock and collected the gold and gems that were strewn behind as they tunneled. They climbed upon the Rodal and traveled the world in search of bigger and better treasure. The Atmal lifted them high upon the mountains where they could follow the Mountain Gemal through the jewel-encrusted mountains of Budora. They lived in giant caverns, filled with the colorful rocky jewels that they amassed in glorious piles. Through the light of day and the darkness of night, the beings lived on. Such was the way for many millennia until the time of the Great Burning.

"While the Prieran Beasts had no mind or will, the Valazen had immense intellect and cunning, and were intuitively competitive to collect the bigger piles of gems for Coveal and Mindal and the Eminent Mother. The brothers enjoyed their subservience, and the Valazen took allegiance with the Lightness of Mindal, the Darkness of Coveal. Others felt their allegiance should be to neither the light nor the dark but to the Eminent Mother herself.

"The Valazen did little to end the struggles between Mindal and Coveal. Coveal was finally driven to madness by his envy of the Great Beasts and their treasures, and his failed attempts to darken Budora were thwarted time after time by Mindal. His envy turned into jealousy and jealousy into resentment and resentment into anger. His anger raged within and drove him to destroy Budora rather than share it with his protective brother of light. From the depths of darkness of the skies he pulled an enormous black moon and hurled it at Budora and covered the jeweled rock with sable mud and dirt. He then drew two fiery stars from his mother's sky and launched them with all his might, setting the mud aflame all over the world.

"Mindal pushed Coveal to the furthest most skies and turned to the sweet jewel of Budora but saw nothing but a mud caked rock. The Great Jewel had become no more than a sullied stone. Mindal continued to push Coveal.

"The Prieran Beasts struggled to survive but died quickly. The Flotal were buried helplessly under the mud and as they died their bodies melted and became the rivers and seas of Budora filled with the watery magic of Flotal. The Atmal expired into air, giving the magic breath of life to Budora. Gemal expired *into rock and filled it with magic. The Rodal expired into wood for the fires of Budora.*

"The Eminent Mother looked upon blazing Budora with sadness. In a single angry breath, she extinguished the Burning Jewel and punished her sons by killing them and affixed their ethereal forms to the dead Budora as the sun and moon to live eternally lighting and darkening the muddied land they had made of her glorious gift.

"Only nine of the Valazen survived the Burning Jewel. The heartbroken Eminent Mother, her sons now gone, breathed one last magical breath of conception into the surviving Valazen and expired into the winds.

"And so it was the Valazen, bestowed anew with the gift of creation, which began the creation of mortal life on Budora."

Gweutan-ven took a long deep breath and paused. No one else in the room even moved. The Elven version had become, through its many revisions and rewritings, simply a chronology of events, and for what Gweutan-ven had read thus far, only three entries were made. Creation, Destruction, and the Valazen rise to power. After which there is much chronology of the creation of the Elves and the history of the Elven City-States, founded by families of Elves. The Human version was such an intriguing story!

Wittig left the seminar that day determined to learn all he could about the Valazen through a Human's eyes. It was only fitting. He stayed in Tesvo-nar for another year, and finally accepted the title of Wittig-ven. After that, he found the Elven libraries painfully devoid of the delicious Human literature that he so craved and he packed his things and found his way over the vast river into the Human empire. 200 years later, he still lives happily among the Humans and has been accepted by them as an Elf, just as he was by the Elves, though he still keeps his ears covered by his hat.

I.   The End of Graycliand

The fierce wind shrieked relentlessly around Graycliand. It drove her to her knees blind and deafened. She slowly pulled herself to her feet against the pounding wind and continued her climb up the mountain. One foot in front of the other, another step forward, and another then slammed back down to her knees as the high pitch shriek of the wind would screech around her.

"Stop! Pleeease!" she screamed, but she could never scream loud enough to overpower the sound of the earsplitting wind. She pulled her tattered shawl around her, but none of her light clothing would offer the slightest barrier from the cursed wind even if it hadn't been torn to shreds by her ten-day flight for her life. The pull on her shawl caused her to get caught by the wind and spun once again back down to her knees bloodying them yet again. Determined to die or be free she pulled herself to her hands and knees and began crawling. Hours passed before she finally reached the final peak of the mountain. She rose to her feet and through her tears and the blinding wind, as a blur at the foot of the grand mountain she could barely see the only comfort she had felt in nearly a decade, pure beautiful green, the Terrali forest.

"Great Va'Treala, please help me, I'm nearly home!"

The green blur in her sight glowed slightly at her hoarse prayer and beckoned her down the mountain.

Without stopping for a breath she began her mad scramble down the other side towards the green. Her heart was racing and she was at the brink of complete panic. The muddy crags were an impossible task and she fell as much as she ran and rolled when knocked silly, but she never stopped. Her entire body was covered with scratches, gashes, bumps and bruises but she was alive and she was free. If she could just get away from the incessant wind, she thought. Occasionally the rough mountain trail offered enough of a flat surface for her to lift herself to her feet and break into a run. She would get just outside of the massive wind tunnel when it would slowly find her and descend upon her again, blinding her and forcing her to the ground so she could barely move. Her only hope was to keep her sanity, keep her balance and keep moving towards the green. Another two days of tortuous wind and she finally reached the base of the mountain. She stood on her shaky, bruised legs and ran frantically into the thick, beautiful meadow that spread before her.

Graycliand had been running constantly for ten days. She knew she wouldn't get far before he had noticed her missing. She hoped that she would at least cross the mountains before he realized that she had been gone longer than the normal day and night she usually spent fetching his herbs and potions from the alchemist. In a day and night she could get into the burned forest at the base of the mountains where few survived. Where, as a Terrali, she might have an advantage.

He was quicker than she hoped and his windstorm spell found her just as she entered the black forest at the base of the mountains. Her panic overcame her shock at his abilities in the forest, and she kept running. She knew the passable trail perfectly but the wind blinded her throughout the forest and slowed her. The journey that for a Terrali was usually one day took her nearly three. It was her seventh day of running when she finally reached the base of the mountain and began her climb – the climb and subsequent descent that she had finally completed as she stood knee-deep in lush meadow grass.

His magic was strong and she knew he could find her, but she continued running. He sent the storm to push her to the ground, weaken her in pain and submission over and over until death would be welcome. Only then would he arrive. She knew that he would come and laugh over her beaten body. He would demand that she beg for her life and beg for his mercy. He would take her back to his keep, beaten and near death, revive her and convince her that she owed her life to him. Then he'd continue her enslavement, as he had done for so many years.

She stopped for an instant and glanced up at the bloodthirsty cloud that was once again descending upon her to engulf her in grey whipping winds. For a single moment she weakly regarded it as a cloud of forgiveness and considered atonement. She had misbehaved; she was the only one with the power to stop the torture. She could kneel and succumb and apologize and all would be done. She buried her face into the crook of her elbow and screamed "No!" She patted her satchel and her fingers ran over the vial of potion.

She would welcome his arrival if she could not continue to fight against his magic. She would use what little life was left to laugh in his face and drink the one potion she did buy at the alchemist; the poison that would bring her death.

If horror could ever become mundane, her cursed life had become so until, unexpectedly, she met a man and fell in love. That was her impetus to begin planning this escape. She tried desperately to keep the two from finding out about each other but her enslaver had become suspicious of her wanderings. Eventually he brutally summoned her with his magic and imprisoned her. She never saw her love again. It took months of begging and promises from her for him to trust her even enough to run his errands outside the keep again. When he finally did, she stole away.

The sun shone down on the meadow making the flowers, grasses and shrubs in the meadow glow with life as they did. Graycliand let a squeal of panic and pleasure steal from her throat when she saw the edge of the forest at the far side of the meadow. She was almost there, she was almost safe, and she was almost home. The forest would shield her from the windstorm and allow her time to hide in her native woods. He hadn't unleashed his demons on her yet, so there was hope.

She paused for an instant near a rock outcropping to catch her breath and looked back at the mountain. She saw the cloud of horror creeping over the meadow toward her. As she peered into the storm her violet eyes widened. No, she thought, no, no, no, not yet. Her heart sunk and she knew it was too late. Down the mountain she saw the black figures creeping, slowly creeping. Dozens of dog-shaped black creatures crept like ooze, darkening the rocky slope under the storm that had followed her over the mountain. Tears flowed into her beautiful eyes. She had lost. In complete despair she dropped to her knees and began digging in that very spot. The earth was soft and thick and she dug frantically. Her fingers dug despite the blood that flowed from them and the wind began again. She sobbed hysterically, screaming at herself to dig faster, faster, deeper, deeper. Finally, as she glanced back to see the black oozing creatures spilling off the mountain over the meadow toward her, she reached into her satchel and pulled out the silver case. She spat upon it with hatred.

She could not destroy it alone; she needed help from her people. So close to her forest she had run out of time. She could at least hide the case, stifling its magic, so he could not use it after her death. She dropped it in the hole and covered it with dirt. Then, with what little energy she had left, she pulled a large rock from the outcropping and covered the hole. The wind whipped around her furiously. The sun was completely obscured by his cursed cloud and the ooze dogs had spotted her.

Her mind focused away from the tiny grave she had dug and towards the forest. The thought of reaching home provided her what little strength she could muster to lift to her feet and move. The dogs were right behind her; she could hear their low guttural panting. One reached her before she could run and wrapped its fluid jaws around her ankle. Its teeth sunk into her sending a fiery surge up her leg and paralyzed her. Her back arched involuntarily as she twisted in the grip of the dog's mouth and fell hard to the ground. She stared at her leg in horror as she watched the blackness of the dog's mire creep up her leg. The dogs surrounded her hungrily. The one that had bitten her lowered itself down on two knees and locked eyes with her. Its dark tongue dripped slimy black saliva as he panted heavily and fixed his ugly stare at her. It spoke in His voice, that terrible rasping voice.

"You shall not live; you shall not die" it hissed. She could not scream, she could not move, she could only watch as the black ooze consumed her body. She twisted on the ground as pain surged through her veins and muscles

"You shall always be mine."

The voice growled from within the slime dog. She reached for her satchel. Her only hope was to drink the death potion and escape an eternity of blackness. She willed her hands to move, but they barely twitched until she finally reached her satchel and pulled out the potion. The dogs, all kneeling, stared as the blackness of their bodies and blood slowly crept over her over her arms, the hand that clutched the potion only inches from her lips. Then the black slime flowed over her throat and consumed her face.

"I shall send for you with the talisman."

The creature's final words faded in a slow rumbling laugh.

Her shape was still Elven but as black as the swarm of dogs that surrounded her. It writhed in the grass in silent pain, the tattered clothing of Graycliand clinging to the sticky blackness. The dogs quietly stood and the swarm moved away from her body that lay on the ground. The dog shapes ran with the cloud back towards the mountain as they began to dissolve. The darkened shape of what was once Graycliand brought itself to its feet and moved in the opposite direction. The dogs and clouds disappeared in wisps of smoke as they ran towards the mountain, and the sun could be seen.

The meadow was once again peaceful and beautiful. Only two oddities remained after the horror of what had occurred -- the lone black shape that disappeared into the trees, and the one dislodged rock that lay on the ground. Graycliand was no more, but she had been lucky. The depraved Elf that owned her and enslaved her for so many years had underestimated her. She was afraid of him but had watched his every move. He did not know she had learned that his power over her emanated from a tiny talisman that hung from his neck chain. She had made a perfect matching talisman from an amethyst and switched them the night before she ran from him. She continued to follow his orders without the magic to compel her to do so. With no magic, his orders to serve him disgusted her, yet she granted him each one without a single moment of hesitation. When he finally retired to bed and she knew he was asleep, she left him note that she had gone for potions. Then she ran. He spent night after night trying to summon her with the fake talisman. Even after his demon dogs captured and changed her into a demon herself, he was not aware that what he held had no magic and no power over her.

II.   *Graycliand's Silver Case*

It was 10 years nearly to the day after the end of Graycliand that Kybrand found himself foraging alone in that same meadow. Alone, he thought to himself, all alone. The other foragers managed to slip away before the tiny herbalist realized he was low on Tuenalian root and made his way to the group of Terrali boys. They all stood on a wide limb near the center of the Terrali tree town called Tarbenlief, together. Niot, the nearsighted, aged herbalist had hobbled out of his shop, and before he could twitch his pointed Terrali ears Kybrand was alone.

He could hear the snickering amongst the leaves behind him. All of them had seen the herbalist coming before Niot arrived and had stolen away into the smaller branches. Typical, he thought. Although he was the brunt of the joke, he laughed right along with the snickers behind him. It was, after all, funny.

"Oh, splendid! I'm so glad you're here, young one," Niot squeaked, "I'm in need of some Tuenalian root to mix a batch of Stibelbane paste. Run along now and get some for me, won't you?"

The question was rhetorical. Niot turned and hobbled back into his clay and straw hut without expecting an answer. From behind branches and bridges Kybrand heard more snickering of the other Terrali boys and grumbled a barely believable grumble. His face was light and happy but his throat was doing the best it could at a hearty grumble. This caused even more snickering and chortling from the hiding places of his friends.

"Good cheer, Kybrand! Enjoy the meadow! I hear it is still sunny!"

"Yes!" came another childlike voice from the leaves. "Don't forget to regrow your path; I hear the even the ample sun can track you back into our forest!"

The snickering amplified and continued as Kybrand made his way down the branches to the village entrance.

Tuenalian root. Why couldn't it have been something deciduous, like Phlaris, or lichen so he wouldn't have to even leave the village or the trees? No, Niot needed Tuenalian root. This meant traveling not only out of the village but out of the forest and into the meadow, where the Tuenalian flower grew in tight bunches in the sun. He made his way down to the base of the village and scrambled down the trunk of one of the giant trees. Once grounded, he placed his hand against the tree and closed his eyes. A slight rustle and a breeze about him and the forest appeared thicker around him. He leaned down and unrolled his little suede boots and laced them up to his knee. He turned and walked a path through the forest to the meadow. The forest was thick around his ankles as he walked his path. As he walked he nonchalantly ran his fingers over the underbrush as he walked. Though his feet trampled the path as he walked, the underbrush seemed to jump right back up behind him hiding his path.

Kybrand's grumbles changed to whistles as he made his way easily through the thick forest and emerged into the lush meadow at the base of the mountains.

Kybrand wandered through the tall grass in his laced boots, ears twitching as he searched for some Tuenalian flowers. He poked through the meadow grass, parting the grasses and searching through the small shrubs. Finally he found a healthy bunch of flowers growing in a bunch. Kybrand forced his dagger into the ground next to the clump and sliced the thick root off the plant. He dug his fingers into the ground and found the main root and pulled. The root of a Tuenalian flower is strong and can grow the length of three elves under the soil and travels close to the surface. Kybrand reached down and grasped the root in both hands and pulled. The root pulled up easily from the soft moist earth, snaking all the way up to a single gray rock overgrown with grass which sat alone on the ground next to the outcropping. He followed the root up to the rock and heaved with all his might but neither the rock nor root would budge. He drew his dagger and lodged it under the huge rock, worked it underneath and managed to turn the rock over. He stood and grabbed the root in both hands, took a deep Terrali breath and gave the root one last pull. It sprang from the ground spraying small rocks and dirt in all directions. One larger chunk shot out of the ground with the force of a slingshot and landed perfectly directly between Kybrand's green eyes knocking him flat on his back. If Graycliand's fallen body had left an imprint in the thick meadow grass for the past 10 years; Kybrand would have been laying directly in it. He'd have fit perfectly, too. His small Terrali frame was the same tiny size and shape of poor Graycliand's right down to the pointy ears and long sinuous hands. His eyes were green though, not violet, and just now they were rolling back into his head.

He groaned shamelessly and groped about for the root. His hand fell on the muddy thing that had taken his dignity and almost his consciousness. He wiped the sticky dirt from it and blinked furiously as he tried to focus his eyes. He expected to find a hunk of granite in his hand and soon realized it was not a rock at all. Indeed, it was a small case, made of silver and tooled with shapes and characters he'd never seen before. He tried to open the case but the hinge was badly corroded. Even with his dagger he couldn't wedge open the case. Kybrand's ears twitched in curiosity. He put the case in his suede pouch and ran back towards the forest to share the find with his friends. Surely they'd be able to open the case. He was halfway back to the forest when he realized he'd forgotten the Tuenalian root he had come there for. He doubled back to the rocks, picked up the root and ran straight into the forest. Had Graycliand's black slime figure drawn a path into the forest 10 years before, Kybrand would have been running directly on it.

III.   *Channel of My Blood*

And at the same moment Kybrand ran back to share his find with the rest of his Terrali village, another Elf much older, much darker and far less innocent opened an identical case. With dark gnarled fingers he pulled a violet talisman from the case and suspended it in front of his eyes. The room around him was dark and disheveled, as though no hand had cleaned it in a decade. Parchments were strewn over a desk as black as the night sky and looked as if it were carved from charred wood. Behind him and all around was shelf after shelf covered with flasks and vials filled with herbs, liquids and crystals and various formaldehyde-preserved animal entrails in various states of decay. The scent of freshly concocted potions and herbal mixes did very little to cover the stench of death in the room, but it did not seem to distract the knurled Elf from his focus on the violet talisman in his hand. He turned it over and over in his blackened fingers while muttering short, harsh phrases. His face, eyes and cheeks were solid and unmoving as his lips slid rapidly over yellowed teeth spewing curse-like phrases at the stone. Louder and stronger the curses flowed through his dry lips. He stared into it as though he fully expected the cold stone to react to his voice. His hand closed around the talisman and squeezed tightly, his head tilted back and his voice raised.

"Tuman te-mulciue, Ata!
Tuman te muloutie, Ata!
Peife'ta ata Nhegel!

Now come ye my apostate"

His dry eyelids fluttered and his voice trailed off. He squeezed harder and waited for a response from the stone. Nothing. Just like every day for a decade, nothing. Yet day after day, he whispered to the talisman hoping for a sign.

With shaky hands he placed the talisman back into its case and uttered as a prayer,

"Channel of my blood
Course strong."

His eyelids closed slowly over his tired eyes. For a few seconds they fought to open but it had been many days he had denied himself sleep and tonight his mind would not win its constant battle over sleep. With sleep came the dream that was slowly killing him.

"Nhegel, spare me, I beg you. I'm dying."

Fruitlessly his eyelids stretched and twitched to open but his mind was already being swept into the dreaded dream. One deep breath and his head fell to the table and his mind belongs to his dream.

His dark eyelids twitched over his eyes but never completely closed. Beneath the lids his eyes darted back and forth stopping sometimes for a few seconds as if his mind was focusing on something, then a tiny gasp and a jolt, then they would dart again in a frantic manner as his dreams escaped the confines of his mind and momentarily commanded his body. His lips moved slightly in a dreamy oration and though not a whisper escaped his lips, a string of drool crawled out of the lower corner of his mouth and stretched into a tiny pool onto his desk. His arms were stretched in front of him, the amethyst obelisk forgery clutched in his gnarled right hand. Slowly a few words slipped from his dream and dripped through his drooling lips.

The Tale of the Terrali Nighthunters

"Ey, Nhegel Ey!
Too thick is thy blood for me,
Too pure was her blood for thee."

In his dream he was walking through a dark city. He felt blanketed by the smell of burnt wood and the buildings looked ready to crumble, blackened by fire. He felt no heat and saw no smoke as though the fire had burned long ago and all that was left was char and ruin. The street crunched under his feet as he walked over the thick layer of cold blackened embers that had fallen from the buildings. It was dark everywhere. Little more than silhouettes could be seen through the darkness. He could see what was ahead of him and around him but did not know where he was going but he kept moving forward.

Around him were many Elves also walking quietly and slowly with expressionless faces. Their skin and eyes were pale and grayish but he knew their blood was red and hungry. He was in a fairly thick crowd of these moving people, each walking alone and staring ahead of themselves, crunching through the dark burned streets.

His blood was pounding through his veins and in his ears and as he walked it felt like it would pound harder faster, thundering through his ears in long low crescendos. He could feel the veins in his neck harden and fall with each deafening pound in his head and he would clench his fists as he walked to stop the pain in his hands from the surge of blood.

As he walked he would stare at the people he was passing. Each would feel his stare and look back at him, locking a momentary gaze with his black eyes. Their eyes would widen and he would reach for them. Quickly, they would look away and move out of his reach. For that moment the blood in his veins would surge into his head and his hands feeling like it would pound its way through his fingers and skull. He would scream and hold his hands onto his face and beg for relief. A few deathly pulses and it would end, going back to the normal deafening pounds he was accustomed to. He would close his eyes and walk forward, ignoring the throngs of passing Elves, avoiding their eyes as long as he could, but it would always happen again and again. The stare, the capture of the gaze, the painful, crippling pound of blood through his hands and head that would make him cry out in his sleep, then back to walking.

This night she appeared in his dream, as colorless as the rest of the Elves, but she was not as lifeless. She moved through the crowd looking around her, gazing with interest at the buildings and people, smiling at times, and spinning around to look at the scenery as though it was a beautiful new place for her. She appeared happy and innocent and did not seem to notice the gloomy set that surrounded her. As he passed her he stared and she stared back. She did not snap away like the rest of them, only stared back at him with her curious bright violet eyes. Their gaze locked and he felt the surge of blood pounding into his hands and head. Another pound and he nearly fell to the ground in pain. He caught himself and reached for her neck to share this thick pound of blood. She gasped as he grasped her neck but never broke her gaze with him. He stared deep into her eyes and clenched his fist over her throat and uttered a curse through his dark dry lips.

"Of Nhegel
Through this vessel flows his river
A river dammed bears no power
Accept this flow and channel his power now

He inhaled slowly and awaited the relief of the pressure of his blood as he stared into her curious eyes. She stared back at him blankly at first, then a smile crossed her lips. And then, a much larger, more painful pound of blood wracked through his arm to his hand and through his head, causing a bit to trickle from his nose. He fell to his knees screaming in pain, losing his grip on her throat. As he lay screaming with his knees drawn to his chest and his head held in his hands, she looked down at him curiously with that tiny smile across her lips. Then she moved away from him into the crowds and disappeared.

He awoke on his desk with his pounding head clenched in his dark gnarled hands.

"Curse Haluc! No more of these dreams shall I have!" Raenick's blood thundered through his weak body, his pulse was slow and thick. Each beat of his heart surged through his body as though it would push his blood out of his vessels, through his skin, pour to the ground and finally give him relief. He closed his eyes for a moment in a silent meditation. He breathed slowly in a rhythm slower than the waves of blood that strained his vessels. Finally he calmed his blood enough to move. His body needed to rest , but with rest came sleep, and with sleep came the dream. Without dreamless rest he would die. He brought his hands to his face and rubbed it hard, pulling his dark eyes open from the bottom as his palms pulled down over his leathered cheeks.

"No more."

Raenick stood from his desk and pulled his dark cloak from the wall and clasped it about his neck. He rummaged through the shelves looking for something of value. He pulled bottles of his Drawings, the pure magical substances that is pulled from the elements and used in certain alchemical mixtures, one by one from the shelf nearly frantically, turning the bottles on their sides and peering inside. He chose a bottle filled with a fine black powder and stuffed it into his cloak pocket and swiftly made his way out his door, through his yard toward the streets of Veldtanil-nar. It was still night in the sky and the warm rain soaked his cloak through.

He reached the edge of his yard and passed through the low gate onto the road. He looked back at his greenstone home. The gardens had overgrown and were crawling over the house, walkways and gate. He sneered at it; even the weeds were lush and healthy. Death had no place in Veldtanil-nar, he didn't belong. His disdain for the perfect weather, the tidy gardening elves, and the general happy atmosphere didn't sway the Veldtanil-nar elves either. He would constantly come home to a neatly manicured garden with edged walkways. Though he'd grumble and lower his head as he walked, he was greeted with smiles and the signature "Day of Great Sun to Ye's" that the elves shared with one another. Nothing could convince these happy elves that he wanted nothing to do with them. He thought of Tirweul-nar and longed for that city. The crowded streets were always filled with dark-skinned Elves and dark buildings. The sound of the crowd and industry was all around, ambient and soothing. He'll go back, let the annoying gardening elves reclaim his laboratory and turn it into another of their beloved, confounded gardens. He decided he would go home -- just as soon as he rid himself of these dreams.

Veldtanil-nar was the largest by land size of the seven Elven City-States, but only third by population. Unlike most of the other Elven city-states, Veldtanil-nar had no walls or gates. It was a beautiful city-state in the center of the continent. Its borders resembled a long serpent shaped state that slithered along the fertile valley sandwiched between the foothills of the Rodalspine and the Flotdash Gorge to the east. The climate was insulated and predictable. The Flotdash river that gushed through the gorge was heated by the gods. Ancient Elven tales say that it is the decaying body of the last living Flotal, still burning in the fires of the burning jewel as it slowly cuts its way into the rock creating the deep canyon it now flows through. The waters were warmer than the hottest bath drawn by any elf, and more pure than a Ven heart. Even the rain that poured down in the dark over Raenick that morning was warm and soaked through his cloak and all his clothing and drenched his dark skin.

The geography of the land created a unique climate that plants thrived on. Nearly every dawn was preceded by a light warm shower caused by the roll of steam from the bubbling canyon river which would end as the great sun rose and took over the sky for the remainder of each day. The result was a long thin stretch of fertile, yet somewhat isolated land that contained the most home proud elves in the continent who kept their land manicured and lush. Raenick walked through the warm showers over the perfectly laid cobblestone roads of Veldtanil-nar as the rising sun began to change the sky from black to blue.

As one traveled through the city-state, the change from suburban to urban was nearly imperceptible as you passed the rural farms and entered into more residential areas. Elven homes were large and spacious, built on enormous plats of green rolling hills. Businesses interspersed with the homes so there was no distinct "downtown." Their homes and gardens were works of living art sculpted upon vast rolling green yards. It was often difficult to distinguish the home from the garden as lush flowering plants and raised gardens were part of the architecture of the homes and businesses. They were shapely, carved and masoned from the indigent pale blue canyon stone with built-in planters resembling giant flower vases, brimming with greenery and flowers.

The Tale of the Terrali Nighthunters

Herbs were the economic mainstay of Veldtanil-nar as the climate was perfect for nearly every sort of plant. Veldtanil-nar was, therefore, the home to the finest herbalists in the land. Raenick was on his way to Groheil, one of the more respected herbalists in town. The sky was still dark and it was raining. The warm rain that fed clean water each day to the plant life in Veldanil-nar was now soaking the black cloak and dark skin of wrinkled Raenick. His dry eyelids blinked away the drops as he stared forth and continued his walk. He despised the clean smell of the city which always reeked of clean rain in the morning and a potpourri of herbs as the sun dried the rain and then drenched the land in its rays. Raenick pulled his wet cloak up against his neck as the sun finally awoke on the horizon.

Raenick grew up as an orphan in Tirweul-nar. The orphanage was situated in the very center of the city and the little orphaned Elves were contracted to the businesses about town and the payments were used to keep up the orphanage. Tirweul-nar elves were greedy, though and the living conditions for the orphans were abysmal. Raenick was contracted to Clewenid, an insane old Elf that taught Raenick how to draw magic from stones. Clewenid was cranky and demanding, and Raenick certainly earned the few credits he did for the orphanage by working hard from sunup to sundown each day. Clewenid seemed to grow older, crankier and more insane every passing sundown. During his lessons to Raenick on Drawing he'd lose his temper at Raenick for not succeeding. Raenick felt he was doing well, Drawing nearly as much pure substance from the stone as Clewenid, but it never seemed to satisfy Clewenid. One day Clewenid finally got so fed up with Raenick, he nearly destroyed his own lab.

"Imbecile!"

Clewenid screamed when the few grains of powder fell from the stone Raenick held in his hand. The dark skin of his neck strained against his the veins that were bulging in his dry, scrawny neck as he bellowed.

"I cannot do all the work myself, I cannot!"

He seemed to be struggling to keep his eyes focused on Raenick as he screamed, Raenick remembered feeling horrified at the look that was on Clewenid's face that day. He went into a complete tantrum, balling his hands in two fists and pounding at his own temples with them.

"Stop! Stop! He's n-not ready!"

He appeared to be focusing on nothing and was clawing at his head. He stumbled about his laboratory, knocking over two worktables and dislodging a shelf from the wall as he struggled to overcome whatever malady he was experiencing. He suddenly screamed once more and dropped to his knees and then became completely still and quiet for what seemed to be hours as Raenick silently watched him. His breathing was labored but deep and slow.

"Go home, now, come back tomorrow."

Clewenid spoke through his hands he held tightly over his face. Raenick placed the failed substance on the counter and wiped his hands on his apron.

"Sir, the lab, it has … ," Raenick was interrupted by the old Elf.

"Fine, fine! Clean it up and go!"

He stood up and locked eyes with Raenick and his hand came up from his side involuntarily and reached out for him. Raenick pressed his young dark eyes shut braced himself for the oncoming clout. Clewenid's eyes widened slightly and he took a deep breath and turned away from Raenick.

"I must sleep, clean and go."

Clewenid left the laboratory and walked through the door to his room. Raenick stayed and cleaned the lab. He was confused but not surprised; this wasn't anything terribly different from the way Clewenid had acted in the past except for the ranting about nothing. That was a new manifestation. Raenick thought about what he should do for the degrading Clewenid as picked up the overturned worktables and swept the floor. He wondered if he should alert someone. He was in the process of convincing himself to wait another day before trying to help Clewenid when he heard the screaming from Clewenid's room. He dropped the broom and ran to the door of his room. Inside Clewenid was screaming in a complete frenzy.

"No! He can't have it! I want it all! My head, stop!"

Raenick pounded on the door. "Sir! Sir! What's happening? Are you all right? Sir?" The screaming stopped dead and Raenick pounded harder. "Sir! What's happened to you, sir?"

After a frightening silence, Raenick opened the door and peered inside. His throat clenched and he gasped when he saw Clewenid standing perfectly still and straight in the center of the room in his black night robes. His eyes were focused directly on Raenick and he couldn't break the gaze Clewenid had on him.

Almost involuntarily he stepped through the door and walked slowly towards Clewenid who was raising an arm towards him. When his stepped within arms length, Clewenid seized Raenick's throat in his open hand and squeezed. Raenick continued to stare at Clewenid knowing he was about to die, choked by this crazy Elf. He could still not break from the unblinking icy glare that Clewenid imposed on him. He could still think but could not move. He wondered what it would feel like to slowly stop breathing and die as he awaited the feeling of the muscles in Clewenid's fingers to tense further and squeeze his throat shut, but that feeling never came.

Instead the fingers kept applying the same pressure to his neck as a sudden wave of energy poured though his hand into Raenick. Raenick gasped as deep a breath as he could and his entire body tightened as the sensation burned through his body. Clewenid began squeezing his throat in slow rhythmic clutches that sent a new surge of the radiating heat through Raenick. He could feel it in every part of his self, from his toes through his heart and in his head. It was as if his own blood was being goaded to race through his veins. His eyelids fluttered each new squeeze of power from Clewenid and he began to feel like his veins were going to burst. He could still not move or break the stare he had with the old Elf or even scream. Clewenid began to gnash his teeth and squeeze even harder causing such harsh rushes of energy through Raenick's body that he began to seize. His mind was still coherent and now he was sure he was going to die. He held his breath and awaited the sweet blackness that would stop the endless surges through his body. A low rumble was coming from Clewenid's throat as he stared and squeezed, harder and longer each time until finally he squeezed tightly and held, cutting off Raenick's breath. A long full wave of power flowed through Clewenid's hand into Raenick's neck and spread through his body. His rigid body twitched in Clewenid's hand a few times and he finally blacked out.

The blackness enveloped his body and mind and then spread around him into the room until it too was pure darkness. The world around him once full of life and civilization slowly faded bit by bit into the pure blackness. All that was left was his conscience which felt nothing. This must be death. In this state he reached out and tried to sense something, anything, the darkness felt so lonely and empty. Then a tiny spark in his conscious and he felt a life form in the midst of the vacuum. He focused his conscience toward it. He shared its sensations and it felt like power gushed through his veins. It was a constant rush of energy that had no pulse and no pressure, just an endless blissful hum. He felt perfect and powerful and was content to spend eternity in this empty dream state with nothing but this sensation.

But his conscience was stripped away, pulled by an unknown force and a low echoing hiss that said the words:

"Thy blood of thy world
My channel to thy world
My world to be."

The voice pounded in his ears and his conscious returned to the world where he had passed out. He was lying on a bench in Clewenid's library. He hadn't died. His throat hurt and his blood still effervesced throughout his body as it would for the remainder of his life. His head was pounding and he felt different. He sat up. He rubbed his raw neck which was tender and hurt. He stood up and tried to shake off the tingle but couldn't. He left the room and was headed for the front door when he heard Clewenid's voice.

"Boy, come here."

Clewenid's voice was sane, calm. He turned and found Clewenid standing in the hall, dressed well and looking far more composed than he had in years. His hair was combed and his face was clean shaven.

"You are Nhegelian now; I've given you a gift. It will guide you through the rest of your days. You must follow its call always. Someday you must share it. It is nothing I need to tell you of now. You will know when it is time and you will know with whom to share it."

He turned and walked to the laboratory. Raenick followed. The laboratory was neat, clean and organized, not like he had left it. Raenick was utterly confused. Who had cleaned up the lab? How did Clewenid suddenly regain his sanity? What was this thick churning feeling he felt in his body?

"How long..."

The blood swelled inside him, choking him and stopping his questions. Clewenid smirked.

"How long were you asleep? Dear boy it has been days. You've just been given the gift of the channel, a new blood flow. Your mind and body need time to become accustomed to it."

He picked up a black stone and handed it to Raenick.

"Draw."

Raenick took the rock and immediately felt the magic flowing through it. His blood hissed in his veins and felt like it was foaming with energy. It wasn't like the blissful flow of energy he had felt in the dream, it was an uncomfortable ebb, as though his blood had was tingling and had no where to flow. He smacked his lips and shuddered trying to shake it off.

"You'll become accustomed to that sensation as I did. It will increase as you feel Valazen power, as is in the rock now. It is channel pooling in your veins. Draw, child."

Raenick closed his eyes and focused on the rock. It looked different than the rocks did before. The magic was so obvious inside it, and so abundant! His blood fizzed in his veins; he could feel it bubbling through his sore neck. His eyes widened and he looked at Clewenid who simply stared back and nodded. He gulped back the froth in his neck and focused again, this time using the sensation to coax the magic from the rock. A few grains fell out to the floor and he felt a gush of blood surge through his veins. It felt good, like the thick soup of blood that was pooled in his veins had thinned and could sail through his body. Clewenid inhaled sharply as if he also felt it.

"Good good! Pull at the magic, free the great beast from the stone, picture it in your mind as your blood swirls through it."

Raenick hardly heard or noticed Clewenid or anything except the rock now. Rich with magic it was, reaching for him. Clewenid began to shake while Raenick took a deep breath and focused harder. He clenched his fist around the stone which crunched and suddenly crumbled in his hand and only a bit of grey dust fell from his palm. He turned his hand over and opened it. In the center of his palm was a tiny pile of deep blue dust.

"Pure Flotish. Perfect, give it to me."

Clewenid handed a glass vial to Raenick who shakily poured the powder into it and handed it back. Immediately he felt his blood still and thicken. It made his throat convulse and he choked, trying to cough away the thick feeling. He fell to his knees and grasped his throat, coughing to no avail.

Clewenid chuckled and turned the vial in his hand. "That was only a tiny rock, imagine what a larger stone would have done to you." He put the vial down and pulled Raenick to his feet. "This is the purest Flotish any Elf can make; it is the gift He's given to you for being his vessel."

"Who?" Raenick choked out the words.

"We must part now, forever." He turned to the shelves that were now neat and stacked. He pushed aside some bottles and pulled out a leather-bound manuscript from the back of the shelf. He flipped through the dry pages scanning them hurriedly.

"Yes, yes, herbs, you will need herbs."

He stopped reading and gazed at Raenick as though assessing him.

"Veldtanil-nar is where you shall go."

He said slowly and nodding. He closed up the manuscript and stashed it behind the bottles.

"Do not return to the orphanage, do not tell anyone where you are going. Do not utter a word of this tonight, to anyone, ever. Go to Veldtanil-nar and make a life for yourself there. Your new gift will be enough to sustain you, you will see."

He put one hand on Raenick's shoulder and again the blood gushed through his body.

"You will feel this bond always; it is your bond with Him."

He squeezed Raenick's shoulder and Raenick felt an icy cold jolt rush through him.

"Now do as I bid, and do not return here until you are summoned."

Raenick somehow knew what Clewenid told him was true and did not question it. He went to Veldtanil-nar and began using his new skill of Drawing. The farther he traveled from Tirweul-nar the more his blood thinned and he felt livable again. Thus he had lived for two centuries in Veldtanil-nar.

Sustenance was easy. In a town nearly made of herbs there were dozens of alchemists. They all needed Drawings to complete their potions. Pinches were plenty to trade with an alchemist for a few coins. He was greedy but cunning. He could make fists full of Drawings in minutes but only shared pinches so as not to stand out as a master drawer. He learned how to further refine and process the Drawings so that the alchemists could use them. This required a lab and equipment which he eventually built. After a time the alchemists began making orders with him and he would make and process everything in his lab. He hired an assistant Elf to help him run orders. He was a tiny Veldtanil-nar Elf named Cardil. Cardil would run his errands and fetch his meals while he worked and studied.

When Clewenid died everything changed again. He was in his lab working on a batch of Red Fireash and his body suddenly jolted into spasm. He screamed and fell to the floor. It felt as though each vein in his body would burst. He clenched his jaw and his fists and shook on the floor as the shockwaves rolled through his veins. His eyes felt as though they would burst from his head if he did not keep them shut tight. Cardil had just arrived at the home when heard Raenick's screams and rushed in to help him. Raenick reached out and grabbed his arm. He felt the rush of blood stream through his arm then his hand then his fingers then toward the open freedom of another body, a fresh vessel to channel the thick blood he had surging within him. Cardil screamed and pulled away and Raenick felt the blood push back into him. Cardil ran from the house and left him lying fetal and shivering alone on the floor.

He slept for two days dreaming once again of pure blackness. This time the blackness felt like a warm blanket around him and he did not grope or search for light. He was crawling deeper into it looking for a darker, emptier place. He could feel the darkness calling him and he knew which way to go. Darkness was all around him. It was beautiful as it swirled and reached for him. Tendrils of darkness would flow around him and through him. He wanted more. Finally he came upon a cold dark tomb, an enormous sarcophagus of pure black polished stone. He felt along the edges and tried to open it. The top would not budge. He spent days at the tomb trying to open it. He somehow knew in his dream that opening the tomb was important. There was something inside he needed and he tried desperately and hopelessly to get it opened. Inside he knew was a deeper blackness than all that was around him. He yearned to open it and bask in the purest dark he would ever know. Void of light, void of sound, void of feeling, what perfection was this darkness. He felt the presence of Clewenid about him, then another presence he did not know, then others. They encircled him around the sarcophagus. There was still no light but he could see their faces in his mind. They opened their mouths and a chorus of low voices spoke.

"It is yours now," they said, almost as one. "Find our words."

He groped around him feeling nothing but the cold sarcophagus stone.

"I hear you and…" Raenick shuddered. "I can feel your presence, you are in darkness more pure than even here." Raenick whispered, "How can I find you?"

"Our words, you must find our words"

Raenick searched about him, falling to the floor and groping,

"Where? Where? Will you help me find the darkness?"

"Our words, all we have done for His freedom and power,"

The voices sounded suddenly angered and desperate.

"Find them!"

Raenick finally awoke on the floor of his lab alone. It had been centuries since he had done this on Clewenid's floor but he knew the incidents were related somehow. His blood was pulsing hard against his skin and he could hear the gushing pounds in his ears and the echo of the voices, Clewenid's and the other's, hissing in his ear, "Find them!"

He saw this as a sign to seek Clewenid's advice once more. He packed a satchel and arranged for travel to Tirweul-nar the next morning. As he stood in the neat cobblestone treats awaiting his carriage he was approached by a still frightened Cardil.

"Dear Eidel, what happened, are you all right Sir?"

Raenick blinked to remember that Cardil had witnessed him in his fit the few nights prior. He was too preoccupied with his dream of darkness to give Cardil a moment's thought.

"Of course I'm all right, do I not look well?"

Raenick glared at Cardil. Cardil stared back at him.

"You look… sleepless."

"I am well, now go, you are relieved of your duties, and I must travel a time."

His blood began pounding in his head again. He reached into his pocket and retrieved a small sack of Veldtanil coins and thrust them into Cardil's hand, it was nearly a year's wages.

"Go, fool, for I grow tired of answering your insolent questions."

Cardil blinked and nodded, turned and left. He was used to the strange moods of Raenick, the sudden headaches, the mood swings, the bouts of dissatisfaction and irritable behavior. The coins were enough to have him forget all of it and he strolled off happily.

He traveled to Tirweul-nar and arrived at the old home of Clewenid. The doors were wide open and there were Elves walking in and out of the home their arms filled with Clewenid's belongings.

"What has happened here," he asked one of the dark-eyed Elves who had bundles of blankets held in his arms.

"Ah! The owner here has died, an accident in his lab, yes. We'll take his goods and share them, we will." The Elf scurried off.

"Died?"

Raenick felt a pang of iciness in his heart and his blood frothed through his veins. His blood had been pushing hard through his body the closer he was to Tirweul-nar and now at the house of Clewenid it was hammering inside his head. He clenched his temples and entered the house.

"Find them! Find them!"

He heard the voices inside the beating of his blood. He walked by the Elves that were swarming the house and made his way into the laboratory. The place was cleaned out well, nothing but a few empty bottles and vials were left on some shelves. He glanced around hopelessly.

"Our words, find them!" His head was crashing with the pressure of his blood bulging through his veins. He fell to his knees and clutched his throat and gasped for breath between the thumps of his heart. He suddenly remembered Clewenid reaching behind the bottles on the shelf for the leather-bound manuscript. He stumbled to his feet and reached for the shelf, sweeping the empty bottles onto the floor. His hand groped about on the back of the shelf until it finally rested on the manuscript. He pulled it and stuffed inside his cloak and ran out of the house. Almost immediately his blood simmered inside him somewhat. It still pulsed thick and hard but it no longer felt as though it were about to burst through his skin. He dropped his head and walked swiftly away from the house. He traveled back to Veldtanil-nar and began reading the manuscript which was written in ancient Valazen script. It was undecipherable but the knowledge of the language did slowly seep through him and he was able to read it. It was entitled:

The Course of the Channel

The manuscript was in two parts. The first section was in terrible condition and illegible. Between the scrawl and script and faded ink, he was unable to read much of it. The end was written a bit more legibly. It was short and concise, a set of lines that could have been a verse. It appeared that the words were inked over more than once to keep the words clear.

The Tale of the Terrali Nighthunters

Budoran death, life beyond the veil
Sing from the shroud Decheiuan life.
To the vessel's song,
The essence flows
From fallen vessels
Decheiuan Life.

Prieren draws, each one pure
Dust of death, dark and cleansed
Haluc's bane, alive and burned
Song of Decheiua, in darkness sing
Dechieu's world to yours.

Call them one, all can hear
Call them all, I will hear
With channel coursed He shall descend
And rule with all darkness for then and all.

The second section was written over thousands of years by each of
the vessel Elves. The script came naturally to him. He read each word
written by Elves that had each been home to the channel during their
lives. All had been Tirweulan, dark skinned and born of Tirweul blood,
both male and female. They lived for nearly ten centuries each and had
studied the magic of Budoran elements. They were all masterminds of
the jewel and deft drawers. Each lived one after the other, scribing their
learnings onto paper and leaving it for the next vessel. The writings
were written as though by only one person referring to himself as "I"
and "the vessel." Other than a bit of difference in the handwriting
styles, there was no other sign that there was more than one vessel over
time. They never referred to themselves by their names or distinguished
themselves whatsoever from the other vessels. They were the eternal
life of the channel, one vessel. Though had Raenick himself been clearer
of mind, he would have noticed that as the years and writings wore on
for one particular vessel through the manual, the more insane and
desperate the writings became. Each wrote about the incessant
pounding in their ears. They would write of the free feeling of their
blood flowing through their veins as they worked with the secrets of
Decheiua. As the madness set in stronger and stronger, the writings

would become illegible, dire and less informative. After a spell of entries like this, the handwriting would change and the new vessel would begin where the last vessel had left off.

Raenick read the writings as if they were his own and quickly became as deft as they each were at commanding the magic of the Jewel. Without Drawing, he could pull the magic about him and command it. He could lift his arms and a wave of black essence would curl from the very dirt beneath his feet and swirl around him. It was part of him, like an appendage that could see, feel and hear everything around it. He could send it spinning for miles and could make it dispatch creatures of the essence, commanding each with his mind.

He discovered that calling magic or Drawing elements caused his pounding blood to flow more freely and the sickening feeling of thickening and curdling blood in his veins would temporarily subside. His blood continued to thicken and any moment without magic would make his temples ache terribly from the pressure of the beating blood. It felt as though his very life was being stretched across the skies, freedom at last from his constraining vessel that housed so much pounding blood. The sensation was intoxicating to him but it also weakened him and his recoveries were getting harder and longer. He began growing mad.

This grew worse as the years passed and he found he could study less and needed to practice more in order to keep from losing his mind. The pressure in his veins was growing constantly and needed a release. The channel needed to flow.

As he learned and practiced, he became obsessed with the song of Decheiua, as did each of the vessels before him. Much of the writings of the vessels were attempting to decipher the song.

Strong be the vessel, for these words are mine. I have discovered the second key to the song of Decheiua. Dust of Death, dark and cleansed. These words speak of the bones of a dead Tirweul. The death is recent and unblessed. Blessed not by word of Meogrim . It is of this shall the dust be made.

Another entry:

I have continued to perfect the Draws. Dust, Song and Draws, I have summoned dark Decheiuan through the channel. The beasts live small and shadowed lives and stay not long in our world. If only my mind were clear I could focus longer have them do His bidding and mine. Strong they are, stronger than living creatures. Their essence flows through me in their time in our world and thins my thickened blood.

The vessels before him had discovered that much of the key to Decheiua and had used their skill in commanding Decheiuan beings and their abilities to draw from the elements to unlock a glimpse at an even greater power, the power to command life. Possession was not as powerful as commanding Decheiuan beings as the mind of the vessel could not be overtaken. But the vessel had discovered the Dust, Song, and Draws of possession.

He would relieve his pounding blood by summoning creatures of essence around him. They were beautiful; so fluid and dark. Raenick found he could summon thousands in one chant, if only his head would stop pounding, he was sure he could summon Nhegel himself through the channel. Haluc's Bane was now the only unknown ingredient

Raenick read this with eager interest. Each vessel had an attendant that they kept enslaved. They could assist the vessel and would not question their work. He scratched through the manual and created an item of enslavement crafted from a stone of pure compressed Drawings with engravings of golden Atmalite down each side. The color was vivid violet and it was perfect. He only needed a subject.

He met Graycliand in the streets that day peddling fresh herbs. He offered her the talisman on a chain in exchange for her herbs which she innocently and readily accepted. He uttered a song of possession as she unwarily donned the pendant and he watched her eyes widen and change to the pure violet of the stone. She was his. He never suspected the touch of Va'Treala in her veins.

Graycliand had served him for nearly a century and a half as his blood pounded through his veins.

A shiver ran up Raenick's spine as he remembered his missing Graycliand. Wretched woman. She betrayed him for that useless human. She belonged to him. He could still feel her soul within his but he wasn't strong enough to find her or command her and his nightmares would not stop. Sometimes the dream was of the black city like the one he had that very night. Other times he would dream he shared her new black slime body. She – they – were trapped in a darkened place surrounded by rock walls. In her slime flesh he felt darkness, rock and an unending choking grip on his -- their throats. Nothing else. Those dreams would end with him pounding and pounding futilely against the rock with his soft slime fists. A decade had passed since she had fled from him and he still was unable to summon her.

His growing madness made his obsession with her even greater. His arm shook uncontrollably as he thought of her. He reached over with his other hand and steadied his arm. He remembered the day nearly a century ago he had reached for her throat as Clewenid reached for his. The feeling of his stretched veins had become so overwhelming he could no longer stand it. It pounded through his head as though it would burst through. Within the sound of the rushing blood that pushed through his ears he could hear the chanting of the vessels.

"Flow, Channel must flow. He must Flow."

He grasped his hair, clutched his head in pain and screamed. Graycliand ran over to help him and as she was trying to get him to his feet he reached out and clutched her throat. He heard the chanting in his rushing blood

"No! No! This one cannot Channel!"

It was too late. His hand had encircled her throat and he began to feel the peace of his blood flowing through his arm into her. Complete release was imminent, he saw it clearly. Her body would forever hold the channel and his blood could flow freely, constantly, always. His grip tightened on her throat and he grinned awaiting her body to finally relieve him of the eternal pounding he had survived for centuries. Her violet eyes were wide and frightened as she stared back at him. She choked at the feeling of the rush of blood into her neck from his hand. But then she squeezed her eyes shut and through her lips a whisper of a word.

"Treala"

A warm soft wind swept through the room and her eyes opened wide. Green they were that night, a horrid green like the green of a Veldtanil-nar garden. Raenick felt a wave of nausea shoot over him and then the sudden backwash of blood rushed back from Graycliand through his arm throwing him across the room against the wall. It felt as though his entire body would burst with the flash of pressure that was sent through him and he screamed again. The chanting in his ears was louder and stronger

"Not die! Call Him!"

Graycliand scrambled back from him on the floor and cowered against the wall. Raenick's arms rose over his head and hundreds of swirls of black essence rose through the floor and began spinning through the room. His arms made wide circles around him calling more and more energy of Decheiua into the world. His blood thinned and flowed as he regained his composure. The room was filled with the black essence of Decheiua spinning and swirling and blowing around him. He took deep breaths and finally stood. With one arm still raised over his head he held his gnarled fingers open, holding the command as he stared at Graycliand. He commanded her to stand and walk to him. He stared at her and snarled as her possessed eyes stared back at him without emotion.

"What was that word you spoke?," he demanded.

His gnarled fingers closed into a fist and the swirling masses of black formed into snakes and fell to the ground slithering about her feet. Graycliand looked confused.

"Word? I spoke not master."

"You said a word! What word did you speak that defied me! You called a magic in this room I have never felt before! What was this word?"

Graycliand simply shook her head with a still vacant look on her face.

"I've said no words, master."

Raenick spit and a guttural sound came from his throat.

"Go then, take your lies and go. Forget this night you shall, you hold no power over me."

Graycliand nodded vacantly and left leaving Raenick to wallow in his anger. Nothing was the same again after that. Commanding her became harder and she began to wander. He sometimes thought he should have ended her life and enslaved another but he was losing his mind to his madness even faster then. Now she had escaped and he had spent the last decade trying to retrieve her.

His kept his head down as he walked through the green city. He needed to get to an alchemist to rid himself of the dreams, nothing would stop him. In his cloak his fist surrounded the package of Drawings he brought with him. The largest package he had ever turned over to a simple herbalist, it was sure to widen the eyes of the unsuspecting herbalist, but he would need such a payment to find an herb to give him a deep sleep.

IV.   The Alchemist, Groheil

Raenick stepped inside the alchemist shop in Veldtanil-nar and handed the package to the young alchemist. Groheil unwrapped the paper package slowly on the wooden counter and noted that the Drawing was a fine pure black dust. So fine was the dust that a wisp of fine dust like smoke swirled up out of the paper as he opened it.

"Oh gracious, m'Eidel! What Drawing is this?"

Groheil quickly wrapped the paper back around the silt like material and tightened the laces. Eidel was the title given to a tradesman in alchemy or Drawing.

"Rodalond, of course, thus the black color"

Raenick sneered at Groheil contemptuously.

"No, no, this is not Rodalond, see here, sir. Rodalond is not black as this that you gave me."

Groheil held the powder against the jars as he compared it to the shelved jars of Rodalond Drawings. None were as black or as fine as the powder in the package in front of him. Groheil tilted the open package paper in his hand and watched a layer of black powder flow like thick ink over the top of the tiny pile creating a curling wave of powder smoke to roll over the top and disappear in a wisp.

"I do not share my Draws in such quantity or purity with any shop, but I am in need of a rare herb."

Raenick glared at Groheil. Indeed Raenick cut his Drawings with dust and dirt in order to keep his skill surreptitious.

"It is Rodalond, amateur, do not make me regret coming here."

"Oh gracious, of course! But so black! I've not seen any so pure or fine as this!"

Groheil attempted to right this awful situation as best he could. Doubtful as he was, his curiosity took him over.

"What herb is it you seek for this, eh, Rodalond?"

"I seek sleep. What herbs have you?"

Raenick was staring so harshly at Groheil it made him wobble a bit as he looked about himself.

"Dear, dear," said Groheil nervously keeping his hand tight around the Rodalond in his hand, "I have a tea of campha flower, very sweet and relaxing"

"No! Do you think I've not tried Campha tea? Do I appear to be completely ignorant?"

Raenick bellowed through his insanity.

"Dear, no, dear dear, no."

Groheil stopped trying to think of the logical progression of sleep aides and scoured his books. He called out names, one after the other, of different teas, herbs, salves, potions. Some that helped relax your body, some your mind, some both. Each one received a scream of "NO!" from Raenick.

"Oh.. oh.. here's something I haven't yet made, but here, let me read this to you. This tincture will stop all visions, real and imagined, leading to a trance-like state. It is a strange one, used only by certain monks in their prayers to clear their mind. Oh no, that won't do at all will it."

"Yes! That I shall take. Mix it for me now!"

"Hmm, yes sir. Let's see here, oh dear, dear dear."

"What is it? Is this something you cannot make? Return my Draw! I'll go elsewhere!"

Groheil gripped the Rodalond in his hand.

"Oh sir, I can make this, I require Ztogrin powder of which I have none. I shall fetch it and mix this for you, I'll go myself to the Dwarven mines to fetch the powder. I need a day."

Groheil turned the vial in his hand again.

"Where did you learn to draw this pure?"

Groheil had always envied the drawers and though most had found their calling at a younger age he wished to become a drawer still. Raenick chuckled slowly as he stared deep into the eyes of young Groheil. He leaned forward until their noses were nearly touching and though barely a gravelly whisper came through his lips, Groheil shall never forget the word "Nhegel" as it slowly crept from Raenick's throat, through his lips and into his soul, sending an icy chill through his very marrow.

He was an alchemist mixing the elemental draws with roots and herbs to make Elven medicines and magic potions that aided Elven lives in almost every way thinkable. City Elves had become quite accustomed to using potions for most every function in their lives. There were salves, potions, powders and pills for healing, cleaning, mending, coloring, strengthening, shining, feeding, sleeping, not sleeping, and even ceremonial incenses came from alchemists. Each of these began with at least one elemental draw which was purchased from an Elf with the coveted Drawing skill. Elves had become so dependent on these alchemical mixtures that the alchemy profession was flooded with young Elves, and the demand for Drawings was growing constantly.

But Drawing was an art not a profession and required an inborn skill and unbridled enthusiasm along with intensive training.

Groheil watched these Elves bring their draws to the shop where he would mix them into some beneficial concoction and often wished he were Drawing rather than mixing. The Drawing Elves always looked at him with such a deep stare that he felt he could see deep within them and feel the depth of their wisdom. He viewed the trade of Drawing as an art that required an intense wisdom that he wanted to share.

Groheil nodded uncomfortably and returned the Rodalond to Raenick with a shiver.

"I promise you, dear man, I shall have Ztogrin by two mornings."

Raenick grinned an awful grin and nodded.

"Then bring it to me."

He turned and left, leaving the priceless package in Groheil's tiny hand.

It was warm outside that night as Groheil walked home but he had his topcoat closed to the top and a scarf wrapped around his neck. When he arrived at home he lit a fire in the fireplace and slept in front of it wrapped tight in a blanket. He dreamed of a dark blackened forest still burning. Smoke was pouring from the trees onto the ground. Wild, starving animals were roaming and snarling, their fur and skin also blackened and smoking.

He awoke before daybreak with a start and drenched in his own sweat. He coughed involuntarily to rid both his mind and throat of the dreamy smoke.

"Dratted powder, I must have breathed it in as I had that dratted package open, how careless of me."

Groheil dressed early and scurried down to the alchemy shop. He was anxious to try Raenick's Rodalond in some of his mixtures. He was sure it would create some of the finest potions the shop had ever held.

He arrived at the shop, put on his spectacles and browsed over the leather-bound books on the shelves muttering.

"Rodalond, Rodalond… let's see here."

The shop had a complete set of ancient alchemy books, as well as newer versions and modern alchemy books. Elves were constantly finding new uses for alchemy and as Elves, were constantly publishing new alchemy books with greater uses and usually more ingredients. The base was always one of the thirteen basic Drawings, like Rodalond, and the uses and effects of the mixtures stemmed from that. Groheil loved reading the ancient books. The mixtures were so simple and basic and their uses so magical. He even tried mixing a few but the ingredients never quite mixed right and never had the effect that the books described. The Elves justified this by believing the books to be as fabled as the Valazen and Prieren themselves.

"Ahh, here we go," he said as he pulled a thin book from the shelves. He blew the dust from the outside and looked at the cover.

The Tale of the Terrali Nighthunters

The Eminent Mother's Gift of Rodalond:
The Great Rodal Beasts
Forever Burned
Into Our Jewel.

The Elven religion believed the basic Drawings to be gifts of magic from the Eminent Mother as her sons ruined the world and the Great Beasts and their tiny Valazen servants were burned into the rock. Budora's elements, the rock, plants and water, were steeped with the magic of the ancient beasts as their bodies decayed into the jewel. Elves had discovered the art of Drawing these powers from the elements thousands of years ago within the temples as prayers to the fallen Prieren and Valazen. Different rocks would yield different Drawings with different powers. The first to be discovered were the nine Valazen Drawings. It was a thousand years of perfecting the art within the temples before some of the Drawers were able to pull the four Prieren Drawings from rock and water.

Thousands of years of Elven logic and analysis and Drawing became like the rest of Elven faith; a science with a fable background. Today, every Elf learned the basics of Drawing in their schools as children just as they learned to read and write and most could draw a bit of magic from the elements when they wished. It was a natural science and faith had little to do with it. But skilled Drawers were rare. Drawing was an art that only a few Elves mastered well and there was high demand for their skills in all Elven communities as the use of alchemy continued to flourish. So slow and subtle was the evolution of Drawing from a blessing to a skill that no Elf would ever notice how weakened the Drawings were today compared to those of the ancient times and thus the reason the ancient recipes would never coalesce the way they should.

Inside the cover the first page of the book was a description of Rodalond itself.

Our shattered friends the Rodal bestow us with their strength and loyalty. Gentle beasts with shells like wood carefully polished the jewel for the Eminent family. High were their shells of six sides and stronger than wood or metal but never marring the surface of the jewel. As is the beast so is the gift of Rodalond with six sides and bearing the gift of strength and loyalty.

Below the description was a drawing of the great beast Rodal, a six-sided turtle-like creature with no legs and no head but hundreds of short, thin tentacles that projected from the six edges of its shell that brushed along the surface of the jewel to aid its sparkle for the Eminent family.

Groheil opened the equipment coffer and pulled out the compound optical lenses. The stem of the instrument was encircled by parallel glass lenses of increasing size that allowed one to see very small items, even those too small to see with the eye alone. He opened the package of Rodalond that Raenick had brought and with the tip of his finger dabbed a few particles on the flat glass of the instrument. He peered through the lenses and adjusted them until he could see the flakes and gasped.

"Six sides, good Meogrim! Six sides it has!"

Groheil was simply astounded. The ancient texts had descriptions of the Drawings but never had the actual Drawings matched the writings like this. This was pure Rodalond. The others he had seen looked like dirt, a rock with black flakes which sometimes looked like they could have six sides if the flakes were chipped from the rock. This that Raenick had delivered was perfect six-sided black flakes without even a speck of rock or dirt corrupting its perfect blackness. Groheil glanced back and forth between the lenses and the ancient text reading and comparing and realizing as though the old faith of the Elves was finding itself within him. He ran his fingers over the intricate drawing of the Rodal and gazed at it as if he believed for certain that the world he lived in was an ancient gem that was scoured and polished by this great beast.

He donned his coat and hat and ran out the door and found his way to the Dwarven mines. It took him the entire day but he found the Ztogrin powder he needed. After sharing ale with the dwarves recounting his good fortune in finding the powder he returned to his lab and made up the tincture for Raenick. Ecstatic, he scurried over to Raenick's home to deliver the potion and with any luck get a view of the lab of a master Drawer.

Luck, it seemed, was on Groheil's side, though it may be arguable whether this was the fortunate sort. Raenick came to the door looking more insane than ever before.

Groheil handed him the tincture and said, "Dear sir, I was extremely successful in finding the Ztogrin needed for this tincture. Oh and the Dwarves were so hospitable! So many ales we drank and talked. They have a name for this powder, you know, they hardly believe in gods, but they called in Haluc's bane!"

Raenick stared at Groheil and a wry grin crossed his tired face. He reached for the tincture but his arm moved past it; toward Groheil's throat.

V.   A Priest of Va'Haluc

Vicar Prinot was a priest of Va'Haluc. It is a title so simple and so much what he dreamed of, yet so far from the truth. A priest of Va'Haluc. At this moment, thirty-five years since entombment of Graycliand's silver case and a quarter century after Kybrand lost his one round fight with it, Prinot was neither priest, nor of Va'Haluc, but that's how he still regarded himself. Vicar Prinot had practiced neither his profession nor his faith for a good part of his life yet would still introduce himself as a "priest of Va'Haluc" if anyone inquired. No one had asked in many years.

Prinot was handsome for a human in his sixties with a tall, muscular build and a full head of hair. His hair had turned white sometime in his post-faith years but he had not even noticed. He had been traveling alone for as long as his memories would allow him. He did not stay in any town longer than a few weeks at a time. In the past thirty-five years he had traveled through nearly every Elven State watching and learning what he could of the elves. He stayed alone in the towns studying the people, their clothing, houses, jewelry, and their eyes. He hoped for some sign of what he sought, but never found it. He learned the Elven language as fluently as he thought necessary and spoke it with a thick, clunky human accent.

The pattern of wrinkles that form on a face can tell much about a person's nature. Prinot was no exception. In the rare instances when he smiled faint lines about his eyes and cheeks struggled to appear. However, when he frowned or concentrated, which he was much more

47

apt to do lately; deep lines appeared across his forehead and between his brows. Those were the lines that marked his face even when rested. The lines of happiness had faded over time.

He sat with a wrinkled brow at a table at a Dwarven pub near Merratte-nar. A silk parchment lay on the table before him and he sketched furiously. His eyes never moved from his work, as he was not sketching something he could see at that moment. He drew from memory. He hadn't drawn a sketch of her in years. That was confirmation that he had also lost faith in his quest. Thirty years ago he would draw her hundreds of times, leaving the sketches in different towns, hoping for word that someone had seen her. He had never gotten even a hint of recognition from anyone, Elven or otherwise. Over the years he had lost hope. His life became focused on traveling and hunting, and little more.

He was the only customer at the pub that day so the plump dwarven barmaid sat at a nearby table watching him. She was fascinated with the fury with which he drew. He did not sketch an outline then fill in details until the picture was complete but instead he began with the head of the Elven woman and drew her completely from top to bottom. Each pointy ear he carefully shaded and shaped, then her long hair, gentle wisps drifting into her face. He spent considerable time on her brows and eyes which, when he finished seemed to stare back at him with as much intensity as he stared at her. Her tiny button nose and small smiling mouth rolled off the end of his coal stick quickly and he began sketching her neck and body. The barmaid was captivated as he drew the flowing skirt and soft boots on the Elf. She stood and moved beside him to watch.

"She's beautiful," she whispered.

Startled, Prinot turned to face her, a round bearded dwarven woman. She appeared older than he but dwarves aged quickly and took on older looks much before humans.

"Do you know her? Have you seen her?" he asked automatically, not stopping to hope.

"Ah, nae, laddy" she answered "I nae know a'y el-fen lasses, ah, tis true."

She struggled with the Elven language but had a better accent than most dwarves in the Elven City-States.

Prinot looked at her and sighed. He ran his fingers through his white hair and continued sketching while the barmaid watched. He had lived the past forty years in the Elven City-States and it had changed him drastically. When he left his home of Hallardstin, he was a young, highly trained, highly spiritual man hoping to live his life dedicated to Va'Haluc.

Like many young men he believed himself better trained than he was and his impatience led him to cut short his training. As a youth in Hallardstin, he had earned an apprenticeship with an enormously learned priest of Va'Haluc, Wittig. Wittig was the most devout priest Prinot had ever met or heard tale of. The elder Elf Wittig knew the Book of Illust Creation better than any practicing human priest known to Prinot. He knew every tale of the Valazen ever told and Prinot was lucky enough to hear him tell nearly all of them. After scores of years as a wandering priest, Wittig settled in the town of Hallardstin to practice his faith.

"Faith and magic are two separate things, dear Prinot. When the great beasts died and melted into the jewel, their magic oozed from their flesh into the jewel itself and into the surviving Valazen.

"Calling the magic out of the jewel, the rocks, water, woods, and air, is simple. Calling magic from the Valazen themselves is more difficult and requires pure faith. They will answer only those in good favor. Begging their favor should not be done except in extreme circumstances."

Young Prinot was enthralled with Wittig, his enthusiasm, his tales, and his magic. He spent every day learning from Wittig and assisting him in his Priesthood. Wittig was always so happy

His early days as a priest were happy and successful. The small villages he would visit in the Kemptaran Empire welcomed him and his teachings with open arms. Indeed, the successes traveled in both directions, for he felt his faith was growing and he was gaining the favor of Va'Haluc. From there, he continued his travels south and planned to share his faith and knowledge with the Elves.

He found the Elves to be much more analytical, though. Unlike the humans he had left, the Elves found little use for the teachings of a priest. They did not ask him to recite prayers or bestow his blessings upon them. Prinot found this to be quite unusual yet he respected the Elves for they took nothing for granted and questioned everything. He often found himself discussing the very existence of Va'Haluc with Elves and he enjoyed the challenge. Even after years of this sort of life and teaching, his faith had not diminished, it had simply changed. Eventually he began to question and analyze the source of his own spirituality and faith. It was when Graycliand vanished thirty-five years ago that his faith completely disappeared.

Now he spent most of his time hunting wildlife and selling the meat and pelts for his keep. He had become an adept hunter, using his black nomatite sword with the dusty shimmer to slay the mightiest beasts. It was the only way he could keep his mind off his loneliness. Some evenings he would find his way to the nearest city and spend time in their libraries. The scholarly Elves libraries were amazingly complete with histories and Elven data. He read everything he could find about Elves and how they lived. Over the years he never completely gave up hope but the vehemence with which he searched for her had subdued.

As time passed he spent more time hunting and less time searching. His hair grew longer, and though he'd shave with a sharpened stoned from time to time, he could never be described as clean shaven. The stubble did manage to hide some of his lines, however. Days, weeks and years passed and he'd become less of a city man and more of a nomad. He managed his inner turmoil over Graycliand down to a simmer and would appear to any outsider to be at peace. Why he decided to pick up his coal stick and draw this day he didn't know but he sketched quickly. Her face materialized on the silk parchment almost perfectly and his heart ached as he looked in her eyes, those beautiful violet eyes.

"Ye are searching for dat lady you draw?" The barmaid asked, startling him once again from his sketch.

"Yes, I search for her" he answered slowly "I don't know that she will look much like this anymore, but this is how I remember her."

He was just finishing sketching her booted feet as she spoke to him.

"Well, I can tell ye, ye won't find her in dese parts" the barmaid scoffed. "She's not de type, and ye drawin' her hair too dark! She has blonde hair! Ye drawin it as if she had sum blackish hair."

She pushed at his shoulder and cackled as though the dark hair was a mistake only a fool could make. Prinot tired quickly of the dwarven woman's attitude.

"No, madam, she had brown hair, dark brown hair"

"Nae, lad, she's a Terrali. No Terr ever had brown hair, 'les' she poured herself a dye on it" The dwarven lady nodded, "Dyed it, she did."

The barmaid picked up Prinot's empty ale glass and put it in the large pocket of her apron with a "clink" as it met the other glasses.

Another dwarf sitting at a table in the back began to bark gruffly at the barmaid. She turned to him and spoke just as gruffly. Prinot couldn't understand Dwarven but the two went back and forth in argument for quite a while ending with a grunt by him and he picked up his tankard of ale and swallowed an enormous gulp. She bustled off to the kitchen still muttering in Dwarven. The foam still coated the man's grey mustache and beard and he made no attempt to correct it. He turned his entire body to Prinot on his stool and he spoke in Elven with an awful accent.

"Don' list'n to dat hag, she's all awash about dem wine-aging elves. Don' none other Elves even buy da foul drink, and I a'drink ale, only ale.," he grumbled into his tankard and swilled another long drink. "Wine, waste o' good fermentin'. And don' you listen none about dem Terrs, she likes tinkin' dey like some kinda rare folk come sell her wine. Dey ELVES, dat's all, ELVES."

He finished his tankard and slammed the glass on the table.

"Woman, it's gone!"

"Terrali?"

Prinot stumbled over his words as he stared down at the picture. There was little information in the libraries in the Elven City-States about Terralis, only a mention as an ancient primitive myth. He stared down at the picture he had in front of him. Graycliand was certainly not primitive, and she lived in Veldtanil-nar. She couldn't have been Terrali. The barmaid came back out and filled the man's tankard with her pitcher of ale then wandered back over to Prinot.

"Jes' lookit 'er boots dere on her feet, tha's wot ye tell it's a Terrali, her boots."

The barmaid nodded arrogantly again.

"Ye sees the way they cut down the sides, like two tongues they are on the fronts and the backs of her legs, and sees how they laced up on the sides?"

Prinot stared down at his sketch. Of course he knew they laced up both sides of her legs, he'd drawn the laces with exquisite detail. The boots, like the rest of the clothing, were hand tailored and fit her form perfectly.

"What of the laces?"

"No proper Elf wears boots like dat but Terrs. Dey not made of leather, dey of soft suede. Dey unlace dem and rollem down so dey can run and climb da trees, and crouch in de forests. Only lace 'em up when dey come outta de forests. I seen 'em, I knows dis. Dey come 'ere and trades me some of dey wine every five years, all of 'em with dem strange floppy boots wit' laces"

She shook her head and continued, this time leaning close to Prinot and whispering loudly

"Dis the only store on this side o' de State that dey come sells 'em to."

"And they claim to be Terrali?" Prinot asked, still incredulous.

"Na, na, dey ne'er say a word 'bot dat, course!" the barmaid gave a hearty chuckle, "I jes' been told by my ma, and her ma 'afore her dey Terrali. Dey jes' looks away ifn I talk so I don' say a word. Nice an' all, dey are, jes' not talkers."

The barmaid nodded her chubby head a few more times then turned to go back behind the bar.

"Wait!"

Prinot began rolling up the silk parchment and stuffing it messily back in his tube. He stood and picked up his belongings. She turned and looked at him with a smug look on her face.

"Where can I find these Terrali Elves of which you speak?"

"I don' know where deys comin' from, only dat dey come and I buy dey're wine."

She turned her small stout body back towards the bar and left Prinot staring blankly at her. The old dwarf grumbled.

"Dey are jes' Elves, woman, he can find them anywhere! Dey are all over dis bloody land, nothing special about them."

Prinot turned and smiled at the barmaid, his faded smile lines making a meager attempt at showing themselves on his face. The barmaid had stopped and was smiling smartly back at him. He could see that she was probably very attractive for a dwarven woman. She was rather plump all over with an especially generous rear. Her face was perfectly round with a bulbous nose, and her chins sported a light beard. She wandered over and gave a teasing slap to her husband's shoulder who just grumbled at her and continued drinking his ale.

"Elves dey are, jes' blasted elves."

She looked back at Prinot and winked.

"She is pretty." She said to him, mildly bemused, "I hope ye find 'er."

VI. Terrali

Prinot stayed at the inn in that town one more night, packing all his belongings into his largest rucksack. He realized how lazy he had gotten in his nomadic state, he had collected many things he did not need or use over the past years. As the years went by, his travels dwindled to last only a day or so at a time, so he never needed to pack himself for traveling long periods.

His plan was to travel back to Tesvo-nar, and find out what he could about the Terrali. His face held new indistinct lines of hope as he made his way through the Elven countryside to the city. Any other reasonable mind would have thought the Dwarf's story to be laughable, but Prinot had found a tinge of hope in it. He had finally become tired of his own complacency. The lines of hope on his face were not new, just overrun by newer lines of sadness, then anger, then hopelessness. They emerged hesitantly as if afraid that they would soon be overrun again if this was but another dead end lead. But something about her mention of the Terrali seemed to bear some truth. He had never seen boots such as Graycliand's before or since. It would do no harm to find these other Elves regardless of whether or not they were truly Terrali.

As horses drawing small Elven carts would squeak and rock past him on the dirt roads, he became obsessed with looking at the boots of the drivers and passengers. So many different styles of boots and shoes did the Elves wear but none like he had drawn on Graycliand. If he saw but one pair on an Elf he would know that her tale was untrue. No one but Terrali wore them, how ridiculous! He became more sure as he traveled toward the city that he'd see a dozen such boots. He was wrong.

Each night of his journey to Tesvo-nar Prinot walked deep into the night, another thing he had stopped doing in his lazy migrant state. Though he still regarded himself as a priest of Va'Haluc, he had long ago stopped spending time outside at night. Night was Va'Haluc's realm. A true priest would cherish nights outside blanketed in the darkness of night. During this journey he'd look into the skies and see the flecks of light that were stars. He searched the sky for the constellations. He once knew and could point out hundreds of them, but now knew only a handful. Each night he could remember a few more constellations. On the fifth day, he found himself feeling that he wasn't completely estranged from his faith. As he walked it became clearer to Prinot how his loss of Graycliand had caused him to forgo all else. He avowed to himself that once he followed this last lead he would return to Hallardstin, find Wittig and complete his education. After this one last lead, he thought, and the lines of hope took another small step in front of the lines of hopelessness.

That night he spent under the stars he had a dream that he was running through a forest of black trees. Their trunks appeared to be burned with fire but they still stood. The forest was thick and everything was black. He felt as though he was searching through the forest for something though he knew not what. It was nighttime and it was dark. He could see no stars through the thick black canopy of burned branches. Around him he could hear voices whispering to him and he listened. They were saying one word over and over in his dream. He couldn't understand it but he knew it was important. Dozens of whispering voices saying the same word became muffled and he tried to focus on one voice to hear the word. More and more voices joined the whispering as he closed his eyes and focused.

Suddenly the voices all stopped save for one and it said "Pheordam."

He began to awaken, but he was so deep in his dream it took a long while for him to climb his way through stages of consciousness. He kept his mind on the word, Pheordam. When he finally awoke he knew he'd never heard it. Odd to dream so vividly of a word, he thought as he rose to his feet and began his walk.

It was another four-day trip to Tesvo-nar through beautiful countryside scantily dotted with Elven farms with lush green forests in between. The villages grew denser as he approached the city and with nine days of brisk walking behind him, he was exhausted. He found a humble Elven Inn in a small village near the city gates and went inside to find dinner and a bed. The Innkeeper was enthralled with him as the Elves always were with Humans that lived among them.

"Welcome to our modest village of Floarta!"

He introduced himself as Dietrel, a round bellied jolly fellow who fussed over Prinot as though he were the only guest that evening. As far as Prinot could tell, he was. Dietrel not only insisted on carrying Prinot's bags to his room, he opened his packs and meticulously unpacked them into the drawers. He talked the entire time. He told Prinot about each and every Human guest that had stayed at his Inn, when they stayed, why they were there, how long they stayed. Prinot wondered whether he would share with him the contents of their packs as well. Dietrel did seem to take a while unpacking Prinot's sparse luggage. Prinot suddenly realized was a hodge-podge of his past religious, civilized life combined with his current nomadic lifestyle. Dietrel did seem perplexed and turned the conversation quickly to Prinot.

"Now what takes a young lad like you to Tesvo-nar?"

The Elves always regarded him as a lad, despite his white hair and line-ridden face. Perhaps it was because he was a lad to most of them. Humans only lived for a century or so, but the Elves could live for nearly four centuries. For most of them any living Human could be regarded as a youngster and they would be correct. Elves never really looked old until they were in their fourth century. Even then they did not age as humans. They never grayed and Prinot had only seen a few that even had facial lines. The only sign that an Elf was in his elder years was a bit of feebleness, a cane, shaky hands, and a change in their voices.

"I am here to visit the temple libraries,"

Prinot gazed back at the man who was at least twice his age, half his size and looked like a teenager at best.

"As you are? Have you completely gone mad, lad? Have you seen yourself? I thought sure it was the mines you were seeking!"

Prinot hadn't seen himself lately. It hadn't occurred to him to find a mirror and look into it. Prinot glanced into the aged mirror over the dresser, shocked. He had become an old man somewhere in the past thirty-some years. Traveling alone for most of his recent past had given him no opportunities to care for his appearance, or a mirror to even look at himself. He stroked his hand over his day-old beard that he'd loosely shaven the previous day.

"I suppose you're right, I hadn't thought of that," he said back to the innkeeper. "Tesvo-nar is quite a civilized city, I suppose I should civilize myself."

"And ye were going to visit the temples! Brilliant Va'Lator, where have you been? If a priest saw you like that he'd surely think you were there to cause trouble!."

Prinot cringed a bit. There were some elves that still felt humans were less civilized than elves, and those elves were probably correct. Since there were very few elves that traveled to the Empire, it was an easy assumption for one to make.

"What business do you have in the temples?"

"I'm Vicar Prinot, priest of Va'Haluc; I've come to spend some time in the libraries renewing my knowledge of some of the ancient writings."

Prinot didn't tell him the truth about wanting to gather information about the Terrali. He had no reason to withhold his intentions, but elves were so pragmatic. While he loved the banter he used to have with the elves about the existence of gods and the logical possibilities of the validity of the tales of the Book of Illust Creation, he only wanted to believe it right now. His faith was so damaged and he needed what little he had to give him a reason to keep searching.

"Dear, dear, supper needs to be set out for the guests,"

Dietrel finally finished unpacking Prinot's effects mumbled something to Prinot about getting "cleaned up" for supper, and scurried off down the hall. Prinot poured some water from an ewer and wiped it over his face. He glanced back into the mirror and brushed his hair back, wondering how he'd make himself presentable enough to go to the temple tomorrow. He wandered back down the hall to the dining hall.

The room was soft and comfortable. The tables were large and round, and there were half a dozen porcelain crocks in the center of each with relishes such as pickles, turnips, sliced carrots, fresh butter and jams. There was a steaming bread basket on each of the tables and the smell of fresh bread filled the homey air of the room. The tables were filled with elves, talking, tearing wedges of warm bread and spreading butter. Comfort. Comfort was not a feeling that he had been familiar with lately. He tracked back in his mind rummaging through it like an attic trying to remember the last time he had felt comfort. Graycliand.

"Prinot!"

Dietrel was immediately at Prinot's arm, jarring him out of his thoughts and guiding him to an empty space at one of the tables. He sat him down in a chair at a table filled with happy Elves. Introductions around the table revealed that the entire village came to dine at Dietrel's Inn each evening, and by the looks of it, Dietrel would have it no other way. Dietrel introduced Prinot as a Priest, which incited an enormous round of conversation amongst the table as the Elves attempted to form logic out of the merger of the Valazen gods and the Human vagabond. Prinot kept his head down and feasted on the quail and yam feast that was set before him and the guests by round-bellied Dietrel.

The conversation did venture away from Prinot and he was able to enjoy eavesdropping again on the unending Elven logic as it weaved and bobbed over subjects such as whether the better way to grow eofel flower, to the clothing found in village stores. Even the conversation was comfortable to Prinot and he found himself feeling consolation in the company of strangers. He barely engaged in the conversation but ate slowly so he would have reason to stay. When finally the last few Elves excused themselves and bid him goodbye, Dietrel cleared the dishes and shooed Prinot off to his room.

Prinot stepped into his room and closed the door. He had had more company and comfort in the last hour than he had had in years. His mind felt fulfilled and exhausted as he fell on the soft warm bed and he fell quickly asleep. The dream this night took him back to Hallardstin, and Wittig. In his dream, Prinot had found a torn shawl. It was black, deep black, black as night. Wittig was scolding him as he often had done Prinot's latter days of his apprenticeship. Wittig was adjusting his cap over his ears as he always did claiming that Va'Haluc only granted favor to those in need and Prinot was gripping the shawl in terror, somehow knowing that his grip on it was important. He woke in the morning in a cold sweat, gasping and clutching his blanket. He lay still for several minutes regaining his composure as he tried to put together his dream thoughts. He rolled the dream over and over in his mind, trying to make sense of it but could not.

He rose and made his way back to the dining room. The room was empty, but Dietrel took his arm guiding him to a table and serving him a hearty breakfast of sausages and cakes.

"You wish to visit the temple libraries, you say? Great Va'Lator, then you should look like a priest, not like a country troll."

The little Elf laughed at his own attempt at humor and his belly shook behind his apron, for who had ever heard of a city ogre? A few whispers of smile lines appeared at the corners of his eyes. Elves faces were so fair and porcelain, they looked young no matter what their age. Lines don't tell stories on the elves like they did on humans.

"Is there a place in the village that a man like me could get a decent shave and haircut?"

"A Priest? Of course!"

The Elf innkeeper Dietrel rolled his eyes and disappeared out the door. Prinot heard the sound of closing doors and out the window he spotted the little Elf walking quickly and purposefully down the little cobblestone road. A few moments later, just as he picked up a thick wedge of buttered iona toast, he saw the Elf hustling back.

"All right, lad, Larabaia awaits you."

Without waiting he cleared the dishes from the table and stood back to allow Prinot to get up. Prinot was still chewing the toast and glanced at the wedge he still held in his hand. The Elf quickly took the toast from his hand and waved him from the chair. A bit dazed and still chewing, Prinot compliantly rose to his feet and followed the Elf down the cobbled road to keep his impromptu appointment with Larabaia.

Dietrel did seem to know his village; Larabaia was able to transform Prinot from a ragged hunter back into a refined gentleman. Working on a human priest was an honor to her. She worked hard and long on his white hair and gave him the cleanest shave he could remember, but never quite seemed satisfied with her work.

"If you've got extra time m'lord, I can fetch some cottae clay and see if I can turn out more of those lines on your face."

Prinot frowned into the mirror and rubbed his hardened hands over his soft shaven face.

"No, believe me, you've done as well as can be, I don't have the skin you do, these lines are just part of me."

"But they make you look so old and saddened, like you've never known happiness."

Prinot stared into the mirror and really looked at himself. He did look old and tired and sad and couldn't even remember the last time he had smiled or laughed.

"You've done a fine job, Larabaia, thank you." He forced a smile but knew it was not a happy one. It mattered not, he was focused on other things.

He returned to his room and sorted his belongings. He wrapped some unneeded items into a blanket and carried them with him into Tesvo-nar. As he closed the door to his rented room, he turned around and the little Dietrel was standing right in front of him, dressed in much more formal attire, including wool riding breeches and a short cloak. He had a riding crop in his hand and a small billed woolen cap on his head. He tapped his crop against his boot twice.

"Now, I haven't been to the temples in a long time. I'm sure you won't mind a bit of company, would you?"

Two more taps as if he was waiting for a response.

"No, no, of course not."

Prinot did wish that he could be alone to research any word about Terrali to rule out that possibility for Graycliand. He wanted to keep an open mind as he read. Having Dietrel reading over his shoulder and voicing the typical Elven skepticism might not allow him the freedom he would need. But Dietrel had already turned and walked out the door hurriedly and was standing on the street looking at Prinot impatiently. Prinot shrugged and followed him.

The streets were crowded as usual with Elves tending to their affairs. A few horse drawn carts rumbled through the rocky streets. The Elves were shopping, selling, meeting, banking, cooking, cleaning, dining and always, as always, talking. Elves never tired of their own logic, and a tinge of a smile came to Prinot's mouth as he remembered the endless discussions he would have with them of the logic of the Valazen.

They made their way through the never-ending blocks of businesses, residences and shops towards the temples. Prinot's mind wandered back to Mentor Wittig, and how sentimentally he always spoke of the temples in Tesvo-nar.

"No other Elven state has nearly as rich of temples as Tesvo-nar!" He would say, "When you go, spend hours at the temple of Va'Haluc! His favor is strong there!"

Wittig had traveled both the Human Empire and the Elven City-States claiming to search for the powers of Va'Haluc. He always claimed that the strongest power he could find was in a tiny domed temple near Hallardstin. While Prinot was his apprentice, Wittig would spend days upon end at the temple. The inside of the dome was lined with diamond-flecked obsidian creating an illusion of a night sky riddled with stars. Wittig would sleep there occasionally at night on the cold marble floor, reaching his dreaming sleep in the comfort of the temple. Wittig said that all ones dreams come from Va'Haluc, so where his favor was strongest, the dreams were clearest.

Often Wittig would return from his nights at the temple refreshed. Other times he'd return exhausted. But he always felt enlightened. Prinot spent a few nights with him at the temple. They'd swathe themselves in all black, ritually bathe their eyes in the font and he would dream vividly. He'd share his dreams with Wittig who could always find a brilliant explanation for young Prinot's dreams.

"Va'Haluc is the keeper of the darkness; his favor is strongest in the dark. The nights are the strength of Coveal taking over Mindal" he'd explain to the townsfolk of Hallardstin, "and malicious Va'Decheiu would use his powers to obliterate the light of Mindal for good if it weren't for our beloved Va'Haluc."

Prinot found it fascinating and comforting that a god would use man's own dreams to communicate. The one thing that he did not forgo, even in his post-faith years, was an appreciation of his dreams. His vivid dreams had become very rare, however, and his interpretations were rusty. Shortly after Graycliand disappeared he began having a recurring dream of holding a beautiful violet jewel in his hand. He'd turn it over and over, loving it and admiring it and feeling as though it needed his protection. Then he'd recall a giant black moon hurling towards him from the skies. He'd always hold out his hand with the jewel in an involuntary reflex to stop it and wake in a panic covered with cold sweat as the black moon would collide with him, covering him in cold, dark, sable mud and wrenching the jewel from his hand. The dreams continued for a decade and stopped suddenly.

Prinot did do as Wittig bid and spent some time in the Tesvo-nar temple of Va'Haluc early in his years in the Elven City-States, but he never found the excitement that Wittig had in it, nor did he ever meet an Elf as passionate of the Valazen as Wittig was. Wittig was an Elven anomaly and he was a wonderful mentor, teacher, and friend.

Prinot and Dietrel arrived at the temple gates and Prinot hesitated. He could not remember when he had been here last, but it was before Graycliand had disappeared. He peered through the gates at the lush green triangular garden that pointed away from the gates to the central temple of Va'Lator flanked by the equally beautiful and only slightly smaller temples of Va'Haluc and Va'Marratt. Dietrel didn't notice the hesitation and went right through the gates and headed straight for Va'Haluc's temple. They walked up the steps through the ornately carved pointed arch doorway into the hall of the temple.

It was beautiful and Elven. Twelve huge round columns in two straight rows created an aisle from the doors to the back of the temple where his altar stood. They stretched from the floor to the ceiling and were inlaid with square-cut sapphires spanning the color of blue from a pale powder blue at the bottom gradually shifting through a sky-blue, medium blue, dark blue to deep indigo at the top, emulating the change from daylight sky to night sky. Each of the columns had a different constellation inlaid at the top of giant white crystals.

The ceiling of the oblong temple arced in three domes, each painted with a scene of Va'Haluc reigning over the night. The Elven depiction of the Valazen was similar to the humans, the Valazen were neither human nor Elven, but a race of their own, with smooth complexions and nearly translucent ivory skin. In one of the dome paintings Va'Haluc was atop Blaenc'Dor, his stalwart white steed, Va'Haluc dressed from jerkin to boot in shadow-grey attire. His face was always gaunt yet calm. His eyes coal black and heavily lidded, and always characterized with a star's sparkle in each eye. In another painting only Va'Haluc's facial features were painted. Barely discernable and swirling into the night sky, the two sparkles of his eyes the only stars. And in the third he was painted standing vigilantly beside strong Va'Lator, king of the Valazen in the light of day. Though not as strong as the king, Va'Haluc was always noble, proud and convicted.

Dietrel had wandered down the corridor to the altar and was standing silently, waiting for Prinot. Prinot gripped the blanket pack tightly against his chest and gazed long into the paintings remembering his past, the excitement, faith, love and loss. His face never changed, not a single line deepened or softened as he gazed at the paintings. He left the blanket pack on Va'Haluc's altar without as much as a word or prayer. He hoped that some one would either find the offering in need, or that Va'Haluc himself might accept them. He'd long since lost any hope that Va'Haluc or any other god would actually be listening to him, but he couldn't carry the extra load so he felt it best to leave it someone else. Dietrel stood just next to him, watching him make his offering.

"Those are half your belongings, why are you giving them away?"

"Just... trying to lighten my load a bit, I may be leaving on a long journey."

Prinot turned away from the altar and made his way back to the door of the temple. Dietrel followed him nearly running trying to keep up.

"A journey? Where? I should know these things! You are my client you know! I am responsible for you!"

Prinot stepped outside the Temple of Va'Haluc and entered the Temple of Va'Lator. The building was immense and semicircular in shape, flat in the front and bowl-shaped towards the back. A straight aisle flanked with enormous sword-shaped columns of marble lead to the altar of Va'Lator at the far end. There the great god had been sculpted into the rounded back wall. His muscular arms stretched out wielding two giant swords. His face was sculpted with extraordinary detail from his curly hair and beard to his strong, yet friendly eyes. He was the strongest and mightiest of the Valazen and ruled the realm of the gods.

Directly under his sculpture was an arch of ivory that lead to the altar of Va'Meogrim, his beloved and devout wife. Through it one could see that the entire room was white, with diffused glass in the windows to brighten the room further. Va'Meogrim was the daughter of Va'Decheiu. She is the artist of life also loyal to the Eminent Mother. With her godly pen she constructed all forms of life on Budora. From Elf to Human to earthworm, she had the sketchpad of life. She blew within every being the breath of life from the Eminent Mother. Her breath is present at every birth of every creature on Budora. Without it no creature would open its eyes and breathe.

To each side of the altar of Va'Meogrim were arches that led to the altars of his two daughters.

Prinot and Dietrel passed through the arch draped with vines of fresh roses into Va'Gharana's altar room that glowed with soft pastel colors and was moist and lush with plant life and the sound of fountains created an ambience that quieted the rest of the world. She was the goddess of the arts and seduction, playful and beautiful; she coaxes the artistic side of each being. The Valazen believed that it was only through passion that an artist's true talents could be discovered.

Therefore she was regarded as the seductress, unable to control her passions and desires. She is believed to have had consorts with Va'Nhegel, as well as some of the mortal life that was created by Va'Meogrim.

"The libraries, m'lord, are back this way! Come, come, this is why you are here, no?"

Dietrel was a typical Elf, Prinot thought, social to a fault, yet primarily interested in knowledge, facts, data, and denying them a moment to simply reflect on their own passions. Prinot stood in Va'Gharana's altar room basking in the glow of passion and seduction. He took a deep breath hoping to feel the rush of passion from the altar but none came. He glanced up at the statue of Va'Gharana. She was carved of rose marble and stood in the center of a fountain. Her image was beautiful and her passion well-defined. She wore a circlet of flowers in her curly hair and seemed to be captured in the midst of a dance. She held her hands in front of her, cupped together above her head, filled and spilling flower petals. Only one toe actually touched the ground with the other knee drawn high in a leaping stance. Her gaze was fixed toward the sky frozen in smile with a look of surprise and elation as the water from the fountain rained down upon her face.

"M'lord? The libraries?"

Dietrel had made his way to the back of the altar room and was opening the door to the library stacks. The room was wooden, silent and solemn, an enormous difference after the lively altar room of Va'Gharana. The door closed behind them, closing out the sounds, smells and lights of Va'Gharana. Long tables were set throughout the stacks between the shelves, and many Elves were sitting about, reading and browsing.

"Now I shall help you with your studies, let me gather some of the books you seek. What exactly is it you wish to gain knowledge of? Shall I start with Va'Haluc?"

Prinot was already walking through the stacks, marveling at the number of books that had been collected by the temple. There were more here than he remembered, much more. The Elves had recently become obsessed with collecting books and literature from all races and from what he could tell this library alone had nearly doubled in size.

Perhaps things can change, Elves had stopped rewriting history and had found an interest in recalling the past.

"I'm..." Prinot stammered and he found himself wondering what Dietrel would think of his true interest. "The Terrali, would we be able to find some knowledge of them?"

Dietrel glanced at Prinot and stared.

"Terrali? The fable of the wood elves? Why we could have stayed in Floarto and had tea and I could have told you most of it! You've not heard it? Is that possible? Tis a story we tell to all children. Every Elf knows this myth! I thought you were here to study, not hear silly children's stories, but sit, sit, and you shall hear the tale from the best storyteller in Floarto!"

Prinot began to protest, but Dietrel was already sitting at a table leaning back and stroking his chin, pondering the way to begin the story. He glanced up at Prinot and patted the table instructing him to sit, which Prinot did.

"Now, now now, let me see, let me see." Dietrel was contemplative and serious.

"You stop me if I go too fast, as the fable has much background and I may miss out on a fact or two."

Prinot doubted that Dietrel would ever go too fast to miss a fact, but nodded slowly.

"All right then, to begin, the fable begins back at the burning of Budora by Coveal. Eh? Yes, that far back. Va'Meogrim bestowed with the breath of life began creating the races we are now on Budora. The Elves, Humans, Giantkind, Dwarves. Ah, yes, the beautiful Va'Meogrim also breathed the Eminent Mother's life into the animals and beetles. Yes, yes, you know all this. We'll move on. And you know too, that Va'Meogrim bestowed the breath of life to Va'Merrate's daughter, dear Va'Traela so that she could create plant life. It is her breath that grows the forests, meadows, gardens and even the sea plants. Together Va'Meogrim and Va'Traela were painting the canvas of life as we see it today on Budora. Ah, yes, quite beautiful, isn't it.

"Va'Nhegel and the other Valazen that were devoted to Coveal before the burning never quite believed in the quest to re-beautify the

Jewel. Va'Nhegel was Coveal's favorite Valazen and prizes his place in Coveal's heart. He believes Budora and its life forms to be his own personal playground, to be teased and toyed and hurt. In his dark mind, life forms can be smothered as easily as created. Darkness is his playground and it is his breath that can take a soul into Va'Decheiu's world. Va'Nhegel is God of Darkness and Death. His form is ethereal darkness like that of Coveal. He surrounds us in night and sadness and is powerless in light and happiness. While Va'Meogrim and Va'Treala painted new life on Budora, Va'Nhegel used death to terrorize the life simply to entertain Va'Nhegel. 'Twas Va'Nhegel that brought evil into our world."

"No, no, you've mixed up Va'Nhegel and Va'Decheiu! An important fact, sir!"

Another slim Elf with a thin mustache had put away his reading and ventured over to listen, and of course, argue. Deitrel seemed thrilled that another Elf took interest in his story; the more tellers the better the tale.

"Come! Come! Sit with us, I'm Dieter and this is Vicar Prinot"

Dieter was out of his chair moving as though he were host of he library as he ushered the pencil-mustached Elf to their table.

The Elf continued, turning to face Prinot.

"Egrium, I am! 'Tis Va'Decheiu, the cursed God of Death who tries to take the final breath from all life on Budora. He was the creator of death, if you will. It was he that preyed upon the mortality of life created by the Valazen. Upon the death of a beloved creation, Va'Decheiu rushes in, opens its eyes wide and steals its soul into the depths of his dark world. From there Va'Decheiu creates life from death! He owns their soul and they live in Decheiua, the blackest most foul place to which a soul should be banished for eternity. Va'Nhegel would have no playground without the creations of Va'Decheiu.

"Only our prayer to Va'Meogrim prior to the last breath can save a soul from the curse of Va'Decheiu, as he scours the world in search of every last breath."

The Elf chuckled as he told this, as though he were reciting but did not believe what was said. Dietrel seemed extremely pleased to have another Elf ready to discuss the fable with him.

"Yes, Egrium, Yes! But the Human Priest knows that already. I am trying to tell the fable of the Terrali and perhaps may have to hurry over a fact or two."

Egrium grinned and nodded emphatically and sat, ready to challenge and supplement the story. Dietrel nodded and continued.

"Yes, now, during the beginning days as you know there was residue tension between the Valazen, between those were loyal to Coveal and those who were loyal to Mindal. Va'Meogrim and Va'Treala tirelessly breathed life into the Budora while Va'Decheiu took their last breaths and Va'Nhegel used the Dechieua to terrorize the nights. This went on as you know, until Va'Lator finally stepped forward as King of the Valazen, put his foot down and brought a bit of order to the chaos."

Another chuckle came from the table beside them.

"You make it sound as though Va'Lator simply waved his hand and created order!"

A third Elf stood and joined them at their table, and Dietrel could barely hide his excitement at the controversy there in the temple libraries. Prinot had heard and contended these facts before, over and over, and in his earlier days would have loved to hear a long discussion. Today he wanted them to get on with it. He began to glance around wondering if the Elves would even notice if he stood and browsed the library while they argued. The new Elf was going on again, addressing Prinot.

"Jeimaliyo am I! Yes! Va'Lator was given his rights as King of the Valazen by the Eminent Mother herself before she left. She gave him directly the instructions to keep care of the Budora and bring it back to its Jewel state, and that she would return someday to reclaim the Jewel."

"No, good man, Va'Lator had to earn his respect with the Valazen. Though she may have given him those words, he was still the strongest and the mightiest warrior of them all. Even Va'Nhegel and Va'Dechieu would not cross his words.," added Egrium as two additional elves joined their chatty table. Prinot interrupted them.

"Dietrel, the Terrali, tell me of the Terrali."

"Oh, right, yes, right."

Dietrel strummed his fingers on his coat and thought some more. Prinot imagined that he was scanning the scores of stories he held in his little Elven mind for the best way to segue into the Terrali.

"Oh yes, well. Before Va'Lator took his throne, his wife Va'Meogrim was the most horrified and insulted by the creations of Va'Dechieu and she had a particular love for the Elven race. She commissioned Va'Haluc to protect her creations from the horrors the night which he has done valiantly since that time."

Prinot fidgeted like a child, and glanced around the table, which was now filled with eight chattering Elves, all adding bits and pieces to Dietrel's rambling story.

"All this you already know, yes, yes, on we move. Va'Nhegel was beginning to feel his loss of power as Va'Haluc reigned over the nights. He was beginning to see the power of life that the new races had and envied their allegiances to the other Valazen. He wanted this power for himself and took over the Elven city called Tirweul-nar and kept them rich with wealth and happiness if they would pledge themselves to him. He used his powers and enslaved the Tirweul-nar Elves. He was so much like Coveal, filled with greed and selfishness. He held them hostage and forced their loyalty. Such power he felt from this, but this was still not enough for him. He then wished the honor and respect of the other Valazen.

"Va'Meogrim was enraged that he would use her creations to enhance his feeling of power. She besieged Va'Lator to help her free the enslaved Elves. Va'Lator sent his daughter Va'Gharana to Tirweul-nar to seduce Va'Lator and find the source of his powers so they could break his spell on the Elves and free them. There she stayed with him as his passionate lover and enjoyed her role as queen of Tirweul-nar."

The mention of Va'Gharana and her lust brought chuckles and chortles from the Elves. They had so long ago defeated most of their own passions, and Va'Gharana was an icon of that which cannot be controlled. Dieter continued through the snickers. Prinot tried to appear patient, but he'd not heard this tale of Tirweul, and wanted him to continue.

"Soon Va'Nhegel's lust for power grew and he began to set his sites on other Elven cities. He began making plans to overtake the city of Havenstil-nar, a larger town near the sea. Have you heard of this place, Prinot?"

Prinot shook his head and leaned forward, finally the story was going to become new.

"Yes, this part isn't in many of the books, it's a fable you know, not really factual."

He grinned and kept talking. Prinot did not have to wonder why he had not heard this fable. It was a tale in which the Valazen heavily favored the Elves, so of course it would not flourish in his homeland. And while it would flourish as a children's fable here, most fables were not fact, and were not worthy of an Elves pen. But looking around the table at the group of excited elves, it was obviously a fable they were all familiar with. Prinot had not seen the impact of lore before in the Elves, and this was becoming a very enriching experience.

"Va'Gharana helped him plan, excited that he was to name her Queen of this new city. It was during these plans that Va'Gharana found that Va'Nhegel had betrayed her and had begun a consort with Va'Effeldril, the Goddess of Pain and Suffering. Scorned, Va'Gharana left Va'Nhegel and fled back to Va'Meogrim and Va'Lator and told them of his plans for Havenstil-nar.

"Va'Meogrim and Va'Lator had now lost their patience with Va'Nhegel and knew they had to end to his enslavements. They sent Va'Treala to protect Havenstil-nar and together went to free the Tirweul Elves. Va'Nhegel, in an act of sheer cowardice and greediness, burned Tirweul-nar to the ground and turned towards Havenstil-nar.

"What ensued was pure chaos in the Valazen era. This was the Valazen war that nearly again destroyed the Budora and all life upon it. It was as though Coveal and Mindal themselves had come back to life and fought. The Valazen fought among themselves, building powers of good and evil and using them against one another. You do know of this era, do you not, good Prinot?"

Prinot nodded and helped Dietrel finish the tale of the war. "Yes, it was at this time that Va'Lator finally took his throne and bid the fighting to stop. He demanded that the Valazen retreat to their realms. The Valazen of both Coveal and Mindal all had to agree to stop interfering lest the Budora be completely destroyed. It was time to leave Budora to its new races. He and Va'Meogrim took to their thrones in the skies to guard Budora and the Valazen disappeared. They no longer lived among the races, and now rarely show even their existence. Only a priest in good favor can commune, and even that is rare."

"Yes, but Va'Nhegel never agreed to go and when he did he did not go quietly. Finally Va'Lator and Va'Meogrim wove him a prison out of pure Drawings and the scorned Va'Gharana lured Nhegel inside. Va'Lator sealed the room and Va'Nhegel stays imprisoned and secluded from both our world and theirs to this day."

The Elves grinned and nodded to Prinot as his face became confused.

"But how does this tale regard the Terrali?"

"Oh! Right! Oh haven't even gotten to that yet! Here we go!"

Dietrel seemed surprised once again to get back on track.

"Oh, well, the story goes that to protect them, Va'Treala led the Havenstil Elves into a forest. She breathed life into the forest to protect the Elves, and then breathed the magic of her life into the Elves. She instructed the forest to care for them and make a home for them so they would be protected. The forest did as it was told, growing trees taller than mountains and wider than a town. The elves built an enormous village in the trees! The village is said to have spanned many trees and grew into the skies. These were the Terrali, and they cared for the forest as it cared for them. They called their tree village Emminda. As their village grew so did the trees, growing new branches for them to build on. The forest itself was so dense that no one could enter, save a Terrali. As they walked through their forest their paths were quickly grown over with lush, dense ground growth. The Terrali had plenty of food from the forest as well as shelter; they never had a need to leave. Va'Treala then also disappeared with the Valazen, leaving them to their safe haven of Emminda.

"Emminda flourished and grew for thousands of years." The Elves began sharing stories of the legends of Emminda and the Terrali forest. On and on they told story after story of the villages, the people, the forests and the way of lives of the Terrali. Prinot finally began to realize why the libraries were so sparse on the subject. The Elves were only interested in documenting fact, fables they kept in their hearts and minds to give them opportunities like these to share their stories. His thoughts were interrupted by another of the elves at the table.

"What of the Nhegalian Channel?" the Elf asked. "You must tell of the Nhegalian Channel!

"Oh the Channel, yes. The Nhegelian Channel? Oh indeed that could be part of this fable! There is another part of the fables we call the Legend of the Nhegalian Channel. This fable states that Va'Nhegel, as a desperate measure before he fell into the shadows, grasped a Tirweul Elf by the neck and soaked him with power. The Elf could gain power to Va'Nhegel's Decheiuan servants. This source of power, ongoing and strong, is called the Nhegelian Channel. The Elf was also burdened with a responsibility with the power, the responsibility to continue the Nhegelian Channel. For the Elf to gain use of these powers, he must first identify the next Channeler, should anything happen to the Elf. Va'Nhegel was crafty, and needed a way to leave his mark permanently on the Jewel "

"Yes!" said the Elf, "The legend says that the Elf charged with the Nhegelian channel is so burdened with power, so very sickened with the power of Nhegel, that he himself must channel that power to another. The Elf must choose his successor to the Channel, should anything happen to him. I've heard it told that the awaiting Elf has not in inkling of his impending fate, and that upon the death or destruction of the current Nhegelian, he is suddenly and unexpectedly infused with all the essence of Va'Nhegel, sickened by it, and so the channel has continued for tens of thousands of years. There is also some legend that the Channel itself will usher Va'Nhegel back into our world where he will one day rule us all"

The table was now filled with grinning Elves, all enchanted with the tale and the telling of it. As they smiled to each other around the table, their willing eyes all focused on Dieter who continued. "The

Terrali elves were happy, safe and carefree and stayed within the warm arms of their forest for nearly everything.

"Tirweul also flourished. The burned city was rebuilt by the slaves of Va'Nhegel, as some of them kept their allegiance to him. Their skin was now darkened as is their hearts. One Elf, perhaps him of the channel himself, became quite powerful in summoning the dark powers of Va'Nhegel, and decided to find the Havenstil Elves that Va'Nhegel coveted so deeply and set out to find them. He found their forest easily but since he was not Terrali, he found no sign of their village, nor his the way out of the forest. He was lost, trapped and angry."

"Dear sir, you've left out the part about the forest attacking him," said one of the listening elves.

"Why the forest didn't attack him, it merely taunted him. You know, opening paths for him to walk down, and then closing them. It would grow a canopy so low, the Elf had to crawl. He was hopelessly trapped in the Terrali forest with no way out. Weeks passed and he could not escape. It was as if Va'Treala herself was taunting Va'Nhegel by endlessly torturing his most devout follower. His anger eventually went to madness and he finally fell to the forest floor where he spit out a prayer to Va'Nhegel. There, on his hands and knees, he called on Va'Nhegel to destroy the Terrali. He spat on the ground and a fire began in the forest. Slowly it spread to the surrounding trees and engulfed the village. Eventually the entire forest was ablaze and the Terrali and Emminda were destroyed forever."

Dietrel looked up around the table to see if anyone wished to add anything to his fable.

"That's it? Where are the Terrali now?" Prinot asked.

"Destroyed. But it's a fable, dear boy, only a fable. Sometimes if you walk into a forest, do you not get lost? Elves believe it is the magic of the Terrali still living in the forest. There's no such thing as Terrali, it's a fable, that's all."

"None of it is true? What of the city of Havenstil, did that exist? Anything?"

Dietrel and the other elves shook their heads, amused at Prinot's insistence on finding some piece of truth in the ancient myth. One quiet Elf at the end of the table leaned toward Prinot

"There are some that say that the blackened forest far east of here could be the forest that was burned by the evil Dark Elf."

This brought another round of chortles from the table.

"Aye, I've heard that one too," said another Elf with a grin.

Prinot was now standing and moving towards the shelves, perhaps he would get some useful information from the books as the Elves spoke among themselves.

"Ye are speaking of the Pheordam forest, eh?"

Prinot stopped in his tracks and spun towards the elves.

"Did you say "Pheordam?"

He stared at the Elf that had said the word so clearly, just as in his dream it rang like a bell in his mind.

"Surely dear boy, you haven't been there, it's desolate. Not a living thing in that awful black forest. Neither a plant nor an animal even steps inside it. It's quite dead. No one has been in it or through it, ever."

Prinot shook his head, wishing the Elves would stop talking; trying to remember his dream, but that was not to happen at a table filled with chatty Elves.

"I heard of a chap who ventured to that forest once. He said even the sky darkened as he and his group approached it. Said they didn't get within ten miles of it before they all were sickened. A bad place that. forest."

Dieter nodded to the Elf.

"Aye, 'tis why if there is any truth to the fable, which I doubt, that place would surely fit, wouldn't it, my friend."

The Elves all nodded at this.

"Where is this forest?"

Prinot's voice wavered. The situation had become surreal to him. He had found such a small sliver of hope in something a bearded dwarven woman had told him, and now he sat at a table with Elves that looked less than half his age, stood at half his height, and called him 'dear boy,' telling him that the only thing he had hoped for in decades was a child's tale. Asking where Pheordam forest was brought such chuckles from the crowd that he put his head in his hands.

"Far, far to the east, beyond Planyata-nar." one finally mused towards Prinot.

The Elves kept talking, amusing each other with one horrid story of the forest after another. Finally, hopeless, Prinot stood and left the library. He heard Dieter call after him,.

"Prinot! Don't be late for dinner tonight!"

He passed back through the doors of the temple of Va'Lator and stood in the triangular garden looking at the three temples that stood before him. Huge, beautiful buildings built of wood, stone and metal, so artistically decorated by the Elves whose ability to recall and retell stories was admirable and even romantic. But was that all there is? Fables and stories? Where was the faith? Why should he hold any hope at all when even his own life was simply a series of tales, even the tale of Graycliand?

Prinot sat quietly on a carved wooden bench in the garden and simply stared. It was a crisp fall day and the garden was immaculately landscaped and in full fall bloom. He was surrounded by life, the scent of the flowers, the butterflies and birds fluttering and moving around him, and he was perfectly still. For the first time since he left Hallardstin he actually missed it. He missed how much faith and hope his village had. And Wittig. To Wittig Va'Haluc was as real as himself, and could be called upon by a good priest. Prinot pulled out his sword and held it in his hands. The metal did appear to shimmer with the blessing of Va'Haluc. He remembered watching Wittig perform the blessing. It was spectacular, but did that prove the existence of Va'Haluc? Wittig needed no proof somehow, he simply knew.

Beyond the movements in the garden, Prinot noticed a flickering light emanating from the temple of Va'Marratt. He peeled himself from his thoughts and turned his head to look. The temple was mostly glass, a tribute to the god of the sky and sun. Inside there was some sort of sculpture that was catching the sun in such a way that the light was reflected directly into Prinot's eyes. It was flickering as a lone wispy cloud passed over the sun and now in its absence left a focused stream of light shining across Prinot's eyes. Prinot's curiosity was awakened from his thoughts and he made his way into the temple of Va'Marratt trying to remember what he could of the god of sky and sun.

Devout to the Eminent Mother, Va'Maratt treasured the light that was always present with Mindal. After Mindal was punished and the Eminent Mother left the Budora to the Valazen, Va'Maratt pledged his undying allegiance to Va'Lator to guard the sun, light, and sky. He is the keeper of faith and deliverer of hope. It is his faith in the ultimate return of the Eminent Mother that inspired the rest of the Mindal Valazen to conceive the beauty of life on Budora. It is Va'Maratt that can still communicate with Mindal, the sun. He urges him to shine each day on Budora. He convinces Mindal that when conceding the sky each night to Coveal, to do it in a splendor of colored sky, and to return with the same radiant splendor each morning.

The temple was simply stunning. Light flowed in and around the temple through reflective surfaces on all the columns, statues, fountains, even the benches and walkways were part of the light show. Something in the temple was illuminated in perfectly engineered light for every minute of every day as the sun passed over from sunrise to sunset. Prinot swallowed at the beauty of the temple which he'd never been inside despite his many visits to the temple grounds in the past. The floor of the temple was covered with raised gardens of flowers and succulent green plants. Currently in the temple, the light shone in from above and from multiple reflective surfaces illuminated the statue of a young robed Valazen girl kneeling in a raised garden. Her face was childish and Valazen and she had a happy content look on her face. Her smile was so sincere and full. She appeared to be captured in an effervescent giggle as she reached down with both hands towards the flowers that surround her.

Prinot gazed around the temple looking for the multiple sources of light that caressed this darling statue so perfectly. They came from every direction, from every source, it was truly astounding. Her robe was chiseled will countless facets so the light sources made it appear to sparkle and shimmer.

He walked around the statue admiring the detail and lighting. When he was behind her he was blinded again by a rogue stream of light in his eyes. It was coming directly over her left shoulder. He stepped aside and watched it streamed out of the temple into the triangular gardens directly onto the bench on which he had been sitting. Strange, he thought, everything else was so perfectly carved. He looked again at the shoulder of the girl which indeed appeared to have a piece broken from it.

"The light, it bothers you eh?"

The woman's voice came from behind him suddenly.

"Aye, these statues are so intricately built, she's lost her Dehta. It breaks off once in a while, and I come fix it for her."

The young Elven woman stood beside Prinot holding a small winged statue in her hand. She wore an apron smudged with clay was applying a layer of putty to the bottom of her statue. She climbed into the garden and gently pressed the base of the statue into the child's shoulder. The happy winged being now sat cross-legged on the child's shoulder, arms crossed and wings extended. The rogue light stream had found its home and the sprite was beautifully lit.

"Oh, I.. who is she?"

"This is the child Va'Treala, daughter of Va'Merratt. The baby was consumed with interest in flowers and plants since her birth. I love this little one! I do my best to keep her perfect. I just noticed that her Dehta was a bit askew and now I've fixed it! Can't have her losing her Dehta, eh?"

The woman chuckled and grinned as though she was telling yet another fable.

"Dehta?"

Prinot assumed she meant the little winged figure, but had not heard the term.

"Oh yes, the child Va'Treala always had her Dehta. Haven't you heard the tale? She was her nursemaid and protector. Since Va'Merratt felt he had such duties to the Eminent mother, he charged the little Dehta to watch over his daughter as she grew. Va'Treala was always in the garden creating new and beautiful flowers."

"I know a little about Va'Treala and her role in the creation of plants and trees, but I've never heard of the Dehta."

"No? Well, the Dehta is mostly related to her childhood. There is probably not much written or studied of it, but the good Elves who designed this temple wanted her to be a part of it, and the Dehta is part of her. I only know so much about her since I've taken the job of caring for this temple."

Prinot was completely intrigued by this tiny child Valazen and gazed at her long after the lights had shifted their focus to other surfaces and shone upon another statue in the temple. As much as his faith had waned in the past years, he could not believe it was a coincidence that the light of the Dehta had shined so brightly in his eyes at that moment. He had to find Pheogram. Hope had all but left him and he wanted to keep what little he had left. He walked back to Dieter's inn, packed his things and set out for the east.

VII. The Goblin and the Dehta

Planyata-nar was the eastern most Elven State. It was the largest by area, but had the smallest population. The land was flat and fertile and the Elven farms and ranches were vast. He traveled towards it lazily, catching rides on carts when he could and sleeping under the stars. It took nearly two weeks until he reached the town itself. He passed quickly through it heading east.

The farms grew sparser and the hills grew taller as he made his way east and an enormous mountain range became barely visible off onto the horizon. He was traveling farther and farther from civilization. At some point, the farms became so sparse that it was taking days between farms. He decided to stop at one and seek some advice as to the directions to Pheordam. The farmer and his family were kind, hospitable and far less talkative than the city Elves. Prinot found the family to be relaxed and happy, though they did have severe reservations about pointing him to the death forest as they called it. However, they reluctantly told Prinot to continue east on the road over four hills until the road ended. Then he was to follow the northeastern path over the foothills to the forest.

Prinot and the farmer sat on the porch drinking homemade ale after dinner that night.

"You know, sir," said the farmer. It was nice to be called sir, rather than "lad" or "boy" for a change. "I don't know why any Elf or man would want to visit that forsaken forest, but you seem to have your heart set on it."

Prinot gazed out onto the farmer's fields and nodded slowly.

"So, listen, it's a long way between here and there, and it's getting cooler at night. You'll need food and supplies for a week or so, we're going to fix up a pack for you, all right?"

The question was more of a statement and Prinot's answer wasn't necessary. He was obviously under supplied and he was grateful to the farmer. He'd lived with very little for so many years, but he was never very far from civilization.

"There are only two farms between here and the wilderness. It's best you get stocked up now. Stay here tonight with us and you can be off in the morning. When, or rather if, you change your mind, you come back here and let us take care of you. You sure got a spirit to you!"

Prinot nodded to the farmer and felt just a tinge of trepidation towards the journey he would take.

The farmer's Elven wife had fixed him a pack with more blankets and dried fruits, dried meat and nuts. There was enough to last for weeks, and the pack was heavy. She insisted he wear one of the farmer's warm hand knitted sweaters. He traded his soft hunting boots for a pair of hard rugged climbing boots.

The four "hills" the farmer had described were hardly hills. The road continued over them but they were long and high. They were the foothills to the high mountain range that loomed in the distance. He passed the last farmhouse after three days of hiking and the road ended before the fourth day. Again, the farmer had exaggerated when he described what Prinot would be following as a "trail." It looked as though it was walked upon but not recently. He followed it as the brush and weeds grew taller and thicker beside him.

As he continued hiking the trail became nearly imperceptible and he needed the constellations to guide him northeast. Days of hiking passed and the trees were getting taller and drowning out the brush and weed. It made it harder to stay on track as there wasn't a straight path through the trees and it became harder to see through the canopy into the stars. His mind began to wander along with his feet and he found himself backtracking and feeling confused and lost. Anxiety and confusion took him over and he began believing he was wandering in circles. He decided to gather stones to build little piles so that he could know whether he'd passed the area before. He stacked pile after pile but never saw one again. He was sure he was lost after a few days; he started resting during the days so he could travel at night when the stars were out, as hard as it was to see them.

That night he became so dizzy he had to stop walking and sit down. He slept a few hours that night then awoke to a dizzy nausea that kept him flat on his back groaning the rest of the night. He remembered the chattering elves story in the temple library of a group that had gotten sick and had to turn back. He refused to succumb to this. It had been over a week since he left the farm, turning back wasn't an option. The nausea lightened as the sun rose and it was dusk before he felt good enough to walk again. He continued walking and building piles on his trail. But as nighttime deepened so did his nausea, more violently tonight. He lay under the stars shivering and sweating at the same time bundled in every blanket and piece of clothing he had. His head swam in delirium and in his dream he kept hearing a mischievous maniacal chuckle that would wake him in a start.

Finally the sun rose and his nausea waned a bit. He was able to sit up and make a pot of stew over a fire with the dried vegetables and meat that he had, and even managed to keep a few spoonfuls down by noontime. Feeling weary and drained, but determined that this would pass; he stood and followed his shadow to the east as the sun set behind him. With the sun was setting his stomach cramped violently and he fell to his knees.

Grimacing and clenching his teeth, he spat out, "Va'Haluc, why? Let me find one shred of truth and I'll die happy!," and he fell to the forest floor, drenched in sweat and shaking uncontrollably.

He woke to the sound of arguing. Arguing? Indeed, arguing. Two voices squabbling back and forth. He squeezed his eyes shut then opened them, blinking slowly. The dark sky was just beginning to lighten so he could barely see what was around him.

"You just go away, go on!"

The voice was so high and songlike it soothed him, yet it was small, as if coming from afar. A beautiful warm fire crackled next to him. He moved his arms a bit and found that he was bundled in his blankets. He tried to remember the last that had happened and remembered nothing about bundling properly. He felt weak but no longer sick.

"Hee heeeeeee, go away? And where does you think I am going?"

There was the chuckle he'd heard in his sleep, just next to him. He blinked his eyes again and saw a figure sitting on a log by the fire. It was someone small and thin, not Elven and definitely not human. It seemed taller than an Elf sitting on the log cross-legged with a hand on each knee.

"Anywhere away from him! You horrid nuisance! I told you, I'll not have you stopping this one!"

The songlike voice sounded like it was coming from above him but Prinot saw nothing. He groaned as he tried to sit up.

"He wakes, hee heeeee! How are the bowels this morning?" With each "hee" the figure's back heaved in laughter.

Prinot grumbled as he reached for his flagon of water. The sky was lightening by the moment as he swilled deeply. He was grateful that his stomach felt strong, he needed his energy. He kept his eye on the figure on the log and watched as his features became more visible in the light. His skin was splotchy and greenish, his teeth sharp and as yellow as his eyes.

"Tell me Human, what brings you to my forest?"

The figure grinned at Prinot -- it wasn't a welcoming grin.

"Your forest?"

Prinot drank hard on his water, gulping down the desperately needed fluids and feeling better with each gulp as the sun rose.

"Who are you?"

"He's Goharo, the Rude! That's who he is!"

Prinot scoured around him looking for the source of the melodious voice. Finally his eyes focused on a petite flying figure darting around between him and Goharo.

"He was making you sick just like he always does to our intruders, and I stopped him! Yes, mmm I did!"

"Hee, heeeee, ye not stop me, I stop 'cause I wanted to, I not listen to you, you annoying pixie!"

Goharo stood up and approached Prinot.

"I stop because she want to ask you some questions and she will, and you will answer! But my time this night is near end and I want some answers. Only those I wish pass into my forest, so answer!"

"You haven't asked him a question!" The muselike being fluttered back and forth and finally landed on Prinot's shoulder. Prinot looked at her, blinking. He began to wonder if this was a dream.

"No good sire, it's not a dream. You are as fully awake as I am!"

"Are you the Dehta?" Prinot asked.

To this both Goharo and the sprite laughed.

"Now where, good sire, did you ever hear that term?"

She laughed heartily on his shoulder.

"My name is De'Heatah, goodness how it's been butchered over time since I've been in this forest!"

"De'Heatah"

Prinot repeated in a whisper. He took a rag from his pack and soaked it with water and wiped it over his face, his eyes. When he removed the cloth he blinked some more. Goharo and D'Heatah were still there.

"Speak, Human! Why was you in my forest!"

Goharo glared at Prinot with his yellowed eyes bringing a tinge of nausea back into him.

"I can bring back the illness tenfold on you with just a thought, I've done it a hundred times before."

"Oh stop it Goharo, you insolent goblin. Vicar Prinot is here to find the Terrali, there's a girl he's looking for and he's just not going to stop until he finds her! He loves her you know."

Prinot glanced at De'Heatah and stared, blinking hard.

"How did you know all that? My name? Who told you?"

"You did, as soon as I sat on your shoulder you thoughts were as clear as day. Speaking of day, look at the sky Goharo, sleep well!"

De'Heatah stared from her seated position on Prinot's shoulder across the fire to Goharo. Goharo grumbled and stood up. The sun was nearly up and it was light enough to see him completely. He was long and lanky and hideous. He turned to Prinot one last time.

"You's a lucky Human, say that. That little sprite never stops my fun. It been a lot o' years since I got ta chase someone out. Dunno what gots into her. You's lucky that's all."

Then he walked away and disappeared into the forest.

"Well, I think he listened! Don't you? Don't you think he listened? Oh my, you have no idea what's even happening do you, oh you poor good man."

She fluttered up in front of him and looked him in the eye.

"You've got to move fast! Make your way by day. I'm in charge of days here in the forest, but Goharo plays at night. It's only in dawn and dusk that we have to deal with each other. I think he listened, but he's quite the prankster. You go that way!"

She pointed northeast.

"See the mountains there through the forest? You see the space between the two mountains? There you go, you go walk there! Don't stop now, do you hear? I'll try and make sure he doesn't sicken you again, but you must move quickly."

She fluttered around him packing his pack and refilling his flagon with water.

"Now don't take more than two days to find the Markelews trail. That will take you out of the forest over the mountain. You'll know you're there when you see the burnt tree shaped like Goharo. Go now! Shoo with you!"

"De'Heatah, why are you here in the forest?"

"Shush! And walk! I'll be telling you that while you walk, you must move now!"

Prinot reluctantly, no confusedly, started walking. He glanced back and she had stayed behind, but her voice was in his head. He kept heading northeast watching his shadow.

"Goharo means well, he's just a bit cranky. It really is his charge to keep the forest clear and he does well at it, he's just so grumpy!"

Prinot could hear her voice ringing in his head as though she was right on his shoulder.

"And it's my charge too, and I'm not so bad at it. We shouldn't let anyone see us! When I heard your thoughts and I knew what you were looking for, I knew you had to get through."

Prinot wondered what she meant by get through. He did not need to wonder long, she heard his thoughts and responded.

"By that I mean get to the mountainside, no one is to get there. No one is to get there. No, not anyone shall know where the Terrali are! Not ever! That's what Treala said to Goharo and me before she left! Not anyone!"

Prinot was uncomfortable with how easily she read his thoughts but focused on the word Treala. It worked.

"Treala was my child, no not my own child, but I took care of her, you see. Merratt wanted me to. He made me of the sunlight and sat me on her shoulder. She brought the Terrali here to this forest. They built an enormous city here and then left. Treala took them across the mountains to a safer place. Safe from the Nhegelian Elf that seeks them.

"She left me to guard the city, the empty Terrali city they built as a decoy for the Black Elf. I'd never been away from Treala. She was my child, you know, but she insisted. She left and crossed the mountains and told me to guard the town."

"This was a fable, ancient myths!" Prinot focused on these thoughts so she would respond.

"Oh my yes, it was long ago, but a myth? A myth is a tale is it not? Should it not bear some truth? But I need sun you see, I'm made from sunlight, when the sun sleeps, I do. When the Elf somehow came into the forest and I tried to keep him away from the village, he made much of his progress into the forest at night. Treala made the forest live and I could make the plants grow and hide the village but he was getting closer.

"I couldn't get him to leave but I tried, I did! I only made him go mad and he burnt forest, village and all. Burnt it down leaving only what you see now. A burned forest. But still I must keep vigil, his channel you know!."

Prinot wondered how grumpy Goharo fit into this, but before he could finish his thought she was in his head.

"Goharo the goblin wandered into the forest once. He likes night and he doesn't like the day. He hides at day. Finds a burnt stump and curls up and sleeps. He left his goblin village to be alone somewhere and he came to my forest. I let him stay if he helped me keep the forest clear at night. He's so grumpy and so mean, but not a soul has passed through here since it was burned, no not a soul. Except the Terrali, they only sometimes come through, but that's all. But Goharo doesn't like anyone and will make you sick if you stay, so move along."

"Why have you allowed me to pass?"

Prinot's mind was so filled with questions it was amazing how she could sort through them and find the ones that he was concentrating on.

"When Treala left me to guard Emminda she was very worried about this Tirweul Elf that sought them. She said that his channel was immortal. I was to guard the forest for eternity. She said a priest could help them. I felt something strong in you. I know you can help them"

Prinot stopped. "Them? I only knew her."

"Walk, faster! You won't be there in a day!"

De'Heatah was right; it was more than a day of walking. That night he walked through the night without stopping. Once during the night he felt a sudden pang of nausea that took him to his knees grimacing, he heard the menacing "Hee heeee" from Goharo and then it passed. He stood with a grouse and kept walking. As the sun came up the next day he looked up again to see Goharo sitting on the ground. He wasn't moving so Prinot kept moving forward towards him. As he approached he realized it was a tree stump contorted so fully it looked like the gangly Goharo sitting on the ground. Prinot grunted at it gaining only some satisfaction from it and moved along.

It wasn't hard to find the Markelews trail as it was the only trail in the area that could be climbed. The next morning he began though he was in no way physically prepared for the climb over these rugged mountains. He was never much of a climber and this trail was not what he was prepared for. The rocks were steep and sharp. He had to use handholds most of the climb up, pulling himself to his feet each time he fell. He reached the top of the trail on the sixth day, three days longer than he had hoped and the day he expected to be walking away from the base of the other side of the mountain. He unrolled his quilt and slept right there on the trail that night, hungry. He had eaten all the food that he brought so woke up famished in the morning. Nothing grew on the top of the mountain. Nothing lived on top of the mountain, and there were no certainly other travelers for him to trade with for food.

So, tired, hungry and cross, Prinot set foot down the mountain. The trip down was much faster and easier than the trip up. Once he got going, he did not stop until it was too dark to see his footings. On the morning of the second day of his descent he found a small grove of radish plants, which barely satisfied him but kept him going. That afternoon he could see the beautiful green meadow at the foot of the mountain so he continued to walk as the sun set.

He reached the meadow much after dark, his feet gratefully sinking into the lush grass. In the center of the meadow, he lay out his quilt and fell hard on his back, exhausted. He looked up in the sky and studied the stars. Each star seemed to shine brighter here in the open meadow urging him to spend a few moments finding the constellations. He associated the stars with his lost faith in Va'Haluc, and it seems he had also lost his interest in the stars over the years. He began tracing each constellation with his eyes, but his eyes were heavy and soon he fell into Va'Haluc's land of dreams.

VIII. A Terrali Forest

Prinot slept soundly and peacefully under the stars for hours. He lay still on his back, breathing deeply and steadily until something woke him with a start, and he sat up with a short gasp. He sat still and listened carefully, but heard not another sound save for the few crickets that chirped in the grass. He played the sound over in his mind trying to place it. It was the sound of swift running feet, and whatever it was had run right by him. He thought it must have been a small animal; perhaps a squirrel or chipmunk, and his ferocious hunger overtook his surprise. He snapped open his sheath and pulled out his sword. A bit large for the job, but his hunger was making his decision. He did not have much experience in hunting or stalking small animals, and his large size made him feel a bit awkward, but hunger beats grace, hands down.

He crouched to his knees and turned quietly towards where he thought he had heard the sound. Still he heard no other sound, and he kept absolutely still. Then he heard a quick rustle just behind him. He tightened his grip on his sword and turned quickly, in a sort of ungraceful hop that took him from being crouched in one direction, to being crouched off balance in the other. What he saw surprised him so completely that he took even another hop backwards landing with a grunt on his backside.

Five black-haired elves stood side by side staring at him with wide eyes. They looked quite young, Three men and two women. They were all dressed in dark colors, black, blue and dark browns. They all carried weapons, but they were all sheathed, and their tiny wooden shields were all slung over their shoulders. Their boots all had laces up both sides, and to be sure, they were all unlaced and rolled down to their ankles. They all flinched and gasped quickly when Prinot took his twist-hop-backwards-rump-hop, and took a step back, but they did not run. They just stood staring back at him. Prinot still had his grip on his sword and prepared himself for a fight, if that was what they had in mind. The elves stood staring at him, and he sat staring at them, and no one moved. Their boots, they were Terralis, Prinot thought to himself; they must have been just as shocked to find him here as he was to be awakened by them.

The elves looked so surprised and amazed at him he half expected them to turn and run. Instead though, one of the males smiled amusedly and shoved the smallest male in the shoulder. He ranted something in Terrali, pointing to Prinot, and they all laughed as though teasing the smallest male about something. Even the two women joined in the teasing, and they all chattered in Terrali, as though Prinot was not there. The smallest male simply shrugged and smiled and chattered something back while pulling at his boot and wiggling his pointed ears. Prinot surmised that it must have been the small Elf that had run by him and woke him up, and that made for good humor for the other elves. The Terralis continued to chatter and laugh and Prinot sat and listened.

The Terrali chatter sounded like a flock of sparrows chirping. They spoke with lively animated voices, punctuated with lilting laughter. The Terrali language had many more intonations and inflections then regular Elven language, sounding almost like a song rather than speaking, and in this group's animated state, it was all the more so.

Eventually they stopped laughing at the poor Elf, and turned once again to Prinot. Now they no longer looked surprised, they appeared to be amused, and not in the least bit afraid. Prinot decided it was up to him to say something to them, so he put on his best Elven and said, "Good Eve."

The elves all blinked, and their appearance once again turned to surprise, but only for a moment. It was the smallest Elf who started laughing first, almost choking; his laugh came up so quick. The others followed and the group of them went into a full-fledged belly laughing fit. Their eyes were watering and they were holding their sides doubling over laughing. Prinot, realizing he was in no danger, sheathed his sword, let out a sigh and put his head in his hands. Their ears all wiggled as they laughed and they would wrinkle their tiny turned up noses. Occasionally, one would catch his breath and stand up and turn to the others and say, "good eve," just as clunky as Prinot had, and they'd all laugh again.

Finally, one stood up; the one who had originally given the smallest a shove and stopped the others from laughing. He bowed to Prinot and said, in a much better Elven accent "Good eve sire," which brought only a few snickers from the rest of the group. Prinot stayed seated and offered a small bow back to the elves. He was almost as tall as they were in his seated position, so he thought he would not intimidate them by standing. The truth was that he was not actually worried about intimidating them. He just didn't want to amuse them any further. He was too tired and too hungry to be laughed at any further. Again a silence between him and the group fell.

It seemed that night Prinot was entertain these capricious elves. For as they stared curiously and quietly at each other, Prinot again made the first sound, his stomach growled. Again the chatter began and the amusement returned to the Elf's faces, but they only smiled. The Elf that had spoken to him once before said "hungry" in Elven, and nodded, and the elves all started moving. One female Elf, giggling, reached down and pulled at Prinot's arm. He stood obediently. The others gathered his quilt and belongings and they all started running across the meadow away from the mountain.

Prinot was still so exhausted; he could barely walk, much less run through the tall meadow grass. The tiny Terralis, on the other hand, were as lithe and light beings as he'd ever seen. They were leaping and skipping through the grass with such agility and grace. It appeared more a quiet, yet lively dance. They were smiling at each other and laughing, tossing Prinot's heavy rucksack back and forth between them.

The little female was still holding his arm, as she leapt like a tiny gazelle through the grass, looking back at Prinot and laughing softly. She exclaimed something in Terrali to the others as they ran, and each of them looked back at Prinot, who was barely running, and laughed, pointing at his boots. The heavy climbing boots were yet another form of amusement for the elves, and they were not made for running through grass, so he stopped running. The female Elf ran ahead of him and joined the others in their running dance. Prinot followed them, hungry and curious, into the forest at the edge of the meadow. Just inside the forest, under the trees, the elves had stopped and sat in a circle.

The other female slung a small black long bow off her shoulder and ran silently into the woods. Prinot watched her run across the field and disappear into the forest and never heard a rustle or snap. The others were gathering kindling and small sticks from the nearby area and had built a fire within moments. From their satchels they pulled yams and herbs. They speared the yams onto sticks wrapping herbs around them and laid them in the fire. The archer Terrali returned holding a young forest boar by the hind legs. The other Terralis cheered and laughed, chattering lively congratulations to her. She happily skinned and cleaned the boar, lashed it to a stick, and it too was put over the fire.

The smell of the meat and yams cooking with herbs was wonderful beyond anything Prinot had ever experienced. He had spent two decades in the company of Elves from the city, but these seemed so different. City Elves thought almost nothing of nature. These Terralis seemed to care about nothing except what was around them at the moment. They did not speak much to him, but chattered among themselves in Terrali constantly. Everything seemed to make them smile and laugh. After they had all eaten and seemed much more at ease with each other, the Terralis introduced themselves to him in perfect Elven.

He met Bleithz, the one who had spoken to him first. He appeared to be the leader of the group, but only because he was able to control his laughter better than the rest. He wore a long sheath on his belt, large enough for a broadsword; its black leather hilt protruding from the top. He wore a black canvas tunic open at the sides and tied loosely on either side. His black canvas leggings fit only to just below his knees, laced in the front and slit on either side to above the knees. His boots laced up both sides, but like the rest of them, they were unlaced and rolled to the ankles.

Chantreitta was the Terrali that had taken him by the hand. They told Prinot that she was the fastest runner and the quietest stalker of them. She wore a small shoulder sheath strapped tightly on her back. Her long black tunic was sashed about the waist with a length of black silk lace. She wore black silk leggings down to her ankles, and her suede boots were rolled down. Her black hair was pulled straight back and tied with a leather strap.

The smallest Elf was also the youngest, and, as Prinot learned, the newest to the group, named Kelfaine. He could run the farthest up a tree without his hands and could hide the fastest and best of any in the group. His weapon of favor was his tiny black dagger that he brandished in large "Z's" before Prinot, causing the others to laugh and chatter jeers at him. Kelfaine wore a deep brown tunic and brown suede leggings, which were faded and nearly bare at the knees.

Aewanne was the archer who had stole into the woods and brought back the rabbit. Her green short tunic was so dark it was nearly black. She wore black suede leggings just below the knees, which were belted at the top with a thick leather belt, buckled with silver.

The quietest was Jennser, who carried a black morning star in one side of his belt, and a dark braided hemp whip in the other side. The others said that Jenser could carry the whip in his left hand, and the morning star in his right hand. In one quick motion he would use the whip to entangle the legs of a mountain boar, pull them out from under it, and with the morning star, render the boar dead in one blow. He had straight black hair worn down below his Elven ears, and wore silver stud earring in his left ear.

They all spoke proper Elven, though it seemed to be difficult for them, and their songlike voices were lost when they spoke it. Prinot enjoyed watching them speak to each other in Terrali. Their voices were very animated, and the language dappled with high and low inflections. Their facial expressions and body movements along with the language made their idle chat seem more like practiced theater. He could almost follow their conversations just by watching them. The proper elves of the Elven State seemed so stilted and dry compared to these Terralis. The elves, especially in Tesvo-nar, were focused on studying. Prinot had many intellectual discussions with some of the educated elves about history, the Valazen, the stars and constellations, and the aristocracy of the Elven City-States. While he found the conversations and the elves intriguing and consuming, none seemed to speak with their very souls the way these Terralis did, even in their idle joyful chats.

"Why were you sleeping in our meadow?" asked Bleithz, switching once again to Elven.

Prinot silently pulled the sketch of Graycliand out of his rucksack and showed it to the Terralis. Again the animated colloquy from the Terralis began. They huddled around the sketch, talking and pointing at the picture. They spoke of her eyes, her ears, her clothes and her boots. They seemed pleased with the sketch, studying it carefully.

"Who is this?" asked Bleithz, looking up from the sketch at Prinot.

"Her name is Graycliand, a close ... friend. Of mine, I hoped you'd know her"

Prinot answered quietly. The Terralis continued to stare at the sketch shaking their heads. For the first time, they weren't amused with Prinot; they seemed genuinely concerned for the woman in the picture. "Is she Terrali, could she have come from here?" He asked. He was still tired, and the food and fire were warming him.

They continued to study the sketch, discussing it in Terrali whispers pointing at the clothing he'd drawn with such care. They looked at him, as though appraising him and his intentions.

"This woman is Terrali," Bleithz said kindly, "but we've never seen her in our village or any others."

Prinot thought for a moment.

"Do you think we could take the sketch to your village and ask some others there?"

Again the Terralis amusement with Prinot arose. They giggled and laughed, and made gestures towards him, seeming to remark about his stature.

"You sleep here, m'lord, we'll be back another night. You should not venture into the forest, m'lord, tis easy to be lost."

The Tale of the Terrali Nighthunters

Prinot was amused that these little elves believed he might not know his way around a forest, but he did not argue. Bleithz began speaking in Terrali to the others in a low voice, almost a whisper. They clasped hands around the fire in a circle and together they sung a beautiful prayer in Terrali. Bleithz nodded to the other Terralis and they stood and gathered their belongings. Quickly they all smiled and bowed politely to Prinot, and then they all quietly ran off into the forest.

Prinot was left in amazement at the little elves he had just met. Everything he heard in the library of the temple was true of them, but the Elves did not do justice to the beauty of the Terralis. They were more spiritual than any beings Prinot had met. Prinot lay back down on his quilt and tried to find the stars, but the canopy of the trees was too thick to see the constellations, and the sky was beginning to show signs of the light of morning. No matter, it was only moments before he was again sleeping heavily on his back. He hadn't realized that the Terralis had taken the sketch of Graycliand with them.

He slept far into the next day. When he awoke, the sun filtered down beautifully through the thick leaves of the silwirs above him. He rolled up his quilt and packed it into his rucksack, then tried to plan what to do next. The Terralis had spoken of returning, but he did not know when. He decided to find the village on his own. He began walking into the forest, which was getting thicker and darker with each step. The silwir trees grew close together, and their branches above grew laterally high overhead and intertwined, creating a thick lattice of branches. The undergrowth was lush and dense under his feet, and as far as he could tell, there was no path going through the forest. This forest was different from any he had ever seen. It seemed as though it was virtually flooded with plant life and every plant and tree grew dense and healthy as though it wanted for nothing.

The wildlife was abundant as well indicating that he'd be able to hunt for his dinner. He walked for hours, yet found no sign of a Terrali civilization, or a Terrali person anywhere. As the sun began to set he made his way back out of the forest, and chased down a large quail for his dinner. He did not know how long he could stay here looking for the Terralis, but he was mystified by them and wanted to learn more about this beautiful race of elves. The dwarf in the trading post had said that Terralis had blond hair, yet all of the elves he met the night before had hair black as the night. He had much to learn of them, and he was so curious about them. For the time being he once again lost his obsession with finding Graycliand.

Suddenly he realized he was completely lost just as Bleithz had predicted. He could not find the edge of the forest, nor anything that looked familiar. The plants appeared to grow and change constantly, and he could never seem to get his bearings or even identify a landmark he had seen. He Eventually, after dark, he gave up and spread his quilt on the forest floor.

The Terralis did indeed return to Prinot, arriving completely silently this time, and startling him out of his sleep. They chastised him merrily and lead him back to the edge of the forest to the same campsite they had made the night before. It wasn't terribly far from where he had given up his wandering, and he wondered why he couldn't seem to get his bearings in the forest.

They brought more yams, as well as turnips, carrots and herbs. These they had wrapped in light cloths, and put them in Prinot's rucksack. They brought two large round loaves of bread, one of which they wrapped in cloth and put in his rucksack; the other they broke and shared. They had a light cheese, like goat cheese and a large vessel of Terrali wine, which they said they had made of some berries that grew locally in the forest. Prinot could not remember when he had had such pleasurable company, and he indulged in the bread, cheese and wine.

"We are the Nighthunters" the Terralis told Prinot proudly. "We guard the forest and our village in the night." The Nighthunters were these five Terralis, and while they told Prinot the story of how they earned this noble title, they spoke proudly and sat straight, and not a giggle was heard.

IX.   The Nighthunters

The beginning of the Nighthunters came years ago, when a young Terrali named Kybrand was alone in the meadow on an errand for the town's herbalist. He had stumbled upon a silver case, which he brought home to the village. Inside the case was an oblong talisman cut from a deep violet crystal hanging from a thin silver chain. So deep in color was the talisman that it was nearly black, and slick as glass. It was an eight-sided shaft of crystal, like a tiny monolith, tapered to an eight-sided point on one end. Each flat side was intricately etched from top to bottom with runes which were guilded in pure gold. Kybrand had never seen such an elaborate item of any kind however he recognized that the talisman might be an item wielding magical powers. Terralis generally did not learn much of other languages and writings, so Kybrand brought the talisman to the elders.

Tarbenlief was lead by a group of elders, the keepers of Terrali knowledge and lore. Most of what the elders knew and taught had been passed to them from the elders before them, and for the most part they did not seek out new knowledge. Tarbenlief did have one elder, however, who had spent some time in New Tirweul-nar, Montrealu. Montrealu was quite young when he was bestowed the honor of hierophant by the elders. He had traveled throughout the forest from village to village in his youth, learning the lore and knowledge of many villages. In his travels, he learned the tale of Emminda. Montrealu asked the elders permission to travel to New Tirweul-nar to see if he could learn more of that town or the magic that had destroyed it. He spent many years there, and when he returned, he had changed. He had grown quiet and introspective, and seemed to carry the worries of a dozen Elves. He had not learned much new of the mythical Emminda, but had learned of magic that was practiced by the Elves, and simply told the Terralis that it was best he did not share this knowledge or learn anything further. The Terralis agreed.

However, when Kybrand found the talisman, they called upon his knowledge to help identify the strange item.

The night Montrealu read the runes on the talisman was a dark, clear night. Not even a gentle breeze blew through the village as Kybrand brought him the talisman. Montrealu put on his spectacles and squinted hard at the talisman. He recognized the writings as being of Tirweul descent. He said that the runes of each of the eight sides would invoke a power which could be magical spells, or something more sinister and powerful.

Squinting through his spectacles that perched on the end of his tiny turned up nose; he tried to read the golden runes on the talisman. In his elder squeaky voice, he told Kybrand to hold the candle close to the runes. He could recognize only a few words, which he read aloud. His mouth began moving slowly as he laboriously read the runes. He had spoken only a few words when the wind picked up suddenly, startling the both of them. Soon it died down again, though, and Montrealu motioned to Kybrand to again hold the candle closer. With shaking hands, Kybrand complied.

Montrealu turned the talisman over in his tiny hands again, studying the delicate etched runes. Again he began reading what he could understand with his limited Tirweul-nar learning. The wind began to blow about them again, yet he kept reading. As he read, the talisman began to glow with an intense violet light that illuminated the village. The wind turned into a storm, spinning directly over the village. Montrealu stopped speaking, and mouth agape, stared up at the swirling storm cloud just as a bolt of lightning stuck down onto the branch of the large silwir which Montrealu's hut was built. The branch plummeted to the ground along with the hut and the talisman and the two Terralis fell to the ground.

Kybrand snatched up the still glowing talisman, and put it back in its case and closed the case tight. Immediately the glow stopped, the storm ebbed and the wind died. Kybrand and Montrealu could barely move as the villagers dropped from ropes out of the village to their aid.

At the same time Montrealu read the runes, Bleithz and the others were in the forest gathering sticks and wood for the village. They were still in the thick of the forest near the base of the mountain when, suddenly the wind began blowing around them and they all stopped and looked up into the sky. They expected to see a storm coming yet there was none and the wind abruptly ended.

A few moments later the wind blew again and this time they looked up to see an enormous storm cloud approaching. Afar in the direction of their village they saw a brilliant purple glow shining up into the sky. The group stood quiet astounded at the glow, but that was only the beginning. Soon after the glow began they heard a low moan from behind them.

As they turned, petrified, they saw the black figure of ooze approaching them from the base of the mountain. It was about the same size and height as the Terralis, but black as night, with tattered clothing sticking to it, blowing in the wind. The figure was walking, but with no distinct legs it was more like oozing, slowly towards them, towards the glowing town, hands outstretched, moaning. It was pure black, with no facial features at all, just pure slimy black ooze in the shape of a walking zombie. The Terralis all screamed and stood frozen in fear.

Over the mountain, other black figures were climbing down from the top of the mountain on all fours. Like dogs they were, creeping, no more like flowing, down the mountain. The Terralis stood mouths agape, unable to move they were so paralyzed with fear. Never had any of them seen anything other than forest creatures, and none of them had a weapon readied.

The sky suddenly alit with a stroke of lightning, which appeared to strike directly on the village. And as quickly as it had begun, it was over. The violet glow suddenly stopped, and the black creatures on the mountain disappeared into thin wisps of grey steamy smoke. The creature before them, though, did not disappear. Instead, it twitched as though waking from a trance, and reached for its throat. It seemed startled and confused to be where it was and turned quickly and began to ooze-walk back towards the mountain.

Most of the group could still not think or move quickly, but Bleithz followed the creature. Bleithz caught up to the creature just as it was nearing the mountain, and turned to face it. He unsheathed his black broadsword and in one fluid motion, swung a full swing at the beast's midsection. His sword swung through the black ooze as though the beast was never there, and the beast stood firm as though his sword did not exist. The black beast lifted its arm slowly and swung a wide backhanded sweep at Bleithz. Bleithz was knocked flat as though a hard, cold gale from the top of the highest mountain had blown him down. He felt nothing but pure cold revulsion from the creature, as it turned away from him and continued toward the mountain. He paused in disbelief only for a moment, then cried out for the others to come. Bleithz managed to collect himself and stand, as the others gathered around him.

Together they tracked the creature as it fled into a small cave in the mountain. Though terrified, they worked quickly collecting large rocks from around the base of the mountain, and blocked the mouth of the cave.

Once Bleithz and his crew had returned to the village, the elders called a village gathering. They lit a large fire in the center of the village and gathered to hear of the events of Montrealu and Bleithz. The elders, including Montrealu, sat together at one side of the fire, as they would be the ones to decide what should be done about the plights that had been experienced.

Bleithz told the village Terralis of the black creatures they had encountered near the mountain. The Terralis were terrified, and Bleithz did not minimize their bravery. He described the large evil creature they had blockaded in cave, and the Terralis all huddled together, frightened that the creature would eventually escape and find them. Bleithz also shared with the villagers the one swing he'd taken of the beast. Never had the Terralis heard of such a creature that was invulnerable to the swing of a sword, and this frightened them even more.

The fire settled somewhat as Montrealu told of his experience with the talisman. He pulled the talisman from its case, at which time the villagers gasped and stifled screams. Montrealu remained calm, holding only the chain, allowing the talisman to dangle and turn in the leaping light of the fire. He spoke softly and began telling the Terralis what he had discovered thus far.

He shared that the talisman was designed to manipulate and control someone or something. His knowledge of the Tirweul-nar language and its writings was limited, but that much he could tell. He showed the talisman again, showing that it had eight sides, each of which had a different set of runes etched into the sides. When read aloud, each side has a different purpose. One side identifies the slave. The other sides would serve different purposes, as the maker saw fit. He believed that the runes could find the slave, watch the slave and command the slave from wherever the runes were read.

Montrealu stated that an Elf with such a powerful item would not part with it easily. It was difficult to tell how long the Elf and talisman had been apart but the power of the storm that rose so quickly should stand testament to the power behind it. The runes were Tirweul, he was certain. He was sure that the black creatures that Bleithz and his comrades had met were part of the magic of the talisman. The beast inside the cave would threaten the village as long as the power in the talisman existed. He was also sure that the Elf that had created the talisman was most certainly missing it, and since the powers had now been unleashed, he would certainly come for it. The Terralis shook and cried at the thought of a dark Elf finding their beloved village. No Terrali village wanted to relive the fate of Emminda.

Montrealu and the elders decided it was best to destroy the talisman and its powers. Montrealu said that simply destroying the crystal would not reverse what had already been created, and could indeed cause such a backlash of evil magical power it could destroy the town. Montrealu offered only one alternative. He would need to continue studying the talisman and learn the powers of each of golden runes of the talisman. Once he learned how the powers were invoked, he might be able to write a scroll to reverse them.

The elders agreed, and so it was decreed that Montrealu would travel to Tirweul-nar to learn more of the ancient Tirweul-nar writings.

Still the townspeople were tense. None had ever seen or heard of creatures like the group of foraging Terralis had told that night. Bleithz and his group were considered heroes for chasing off the black beasts, and creating the wall to capture the beast. So revered were they that the group vowed to protect the town from the beasts of the night. The five of then began staying up each night, hunting through the forest watching over the village in the trees above them. They called themselves the Nighthunters.

They had been doing this for many years now, and the black beasts had never returned. The Terralis believe it is because of the Nighthunters watch that they have been safe from evils of the talisman. A few times over the years, Montrealu will be working in his hut to decipher the runes on the talisman it will once again glow and come to life. The winds will begin whipping through the town, and the dull moan from the rock-enclosed cave will begin. The Nighthunters will spring into action, their adrenaline pumping, and will rush to the mountain base to await the black beasts, yet so far, they have never returned. Montrealu quickly snaps the talisman back into its case, and put a stop to the glow and the ensuing storm.

So that is how these Nighthunters came to be. They stayed their time at night hunting the local forest creatures such as the small wolves, boars, small deer, quails, and squirrels. Over the years they began wearing dark clothing, dyed their blonde hair black, and stayed true to their promise to protect the village from the evils of the night. Even though there weren't many evils to fear, the Terralis fended those that were from the town. They were a happy group, and mostly they just enjoyed each other's company.

They had many songs they sang each night about the night and the creatures of the night. Over the next few nights, they'd share them with Prinot. Prinot could not understand the verses they sung, but their songs were as beautiful as their language. His favorite was the prayer they sung every night before the sun rose and they would disappear into the forest. They called this prayer the Nighthunter's prayer.

X.   *The Hut at the Edge of the Forest*

Prinot was curious about the Terrali village, but he had been told by the Nighthunters that only Terrali had ever gained passage inside a Terrali village. He remembered from the table of elves that had told him the legends of the Terrali that once you enter a Terrali forest you may never leave. They spoke of villages could span more than the top of one tree, and that they could be very large and very old.

Occasionally during the day, Prinot would venture into the forest and search for the village. He was beginning to be able to do so without getting lost, as long as he did not venture far. The trunks of the huge silwirs were virtually unclimbable, the lowest branches being the height of three Giantfolk standing one atop the other. He searched through the branches but could never find any sign of the Terralis or their village.

He began sleeping much of the day, and spending the nights in the forest with the Nighthunters. At the edge of the forest, he built a small one-room hut of wood. The Nighthunters helped him weave a hammock to sleep, and brought him a pot to cook. He was quite comfortable, and was in no hurry to leave the forest and these curious elves. He had almost forgotten why he had come across the mountains in the first place.

Prinot was not sure how much of the tale of the talisman and the black creatures were real, but he wondered how these playful Terralis would be able to actually fight off beasts with any real power. They were not afraid at all, but hunting small forest creatures would not give them the training they needed if they ever did need to face the beasts that would come. He decided to stay in the forest with the Nighthunters and assess their hunting prowess. They came back every night to sit with Prinot and tell him their tales. One night, upon their return, Prinot suggested they go deep into the forest and hunt together. This elated the Nighthunters, and they all jumped to their feet and drew their weapons. They began their Terrali chatter, brandishing their weapons and howling into the night.

Prinot was beginning to learn a few of their words, and was able to understand more of their conversation. The Terrali language had a similar structure to the Elven language, and once he had some of the basic words memorized, Who, What, Where, When, How, Here, There, he could hold a primitive conversation with them, picking up the answers to his questions word by word. The Terralis were simply charmed by Prinot speaking their language, they laughed when he would speak and corrected his inflections .They would teach him words as they came across new objects. Prinot found himself smiling more often than he'd smiled in years.

So that night, as they set out on a forest hunt together, Prinot drew his black sword from its sheath; the grey shimmer sparkled in the light of the stars. The Nighthunters gasped at the size and beauty of his weapon. They reached out for it, wanting to touch the grey shimmer that emanated from the sharpened edge of his sword. He showed them the weapon, and for the first time in decades, he taught of Va'Haluc.

"This sword," Prinot began, "is designed in the image of Va'Haluc's holy symbol, and the shimmer reflects his blessing."

Prinot was surprised to learn that the Nighthunters had little knowledge of Va'Haluc, or most Valazen for that matter. Va'Traela, they believed, was the Valazen goddess that had lead the Terralis to the forest to live among the trees, and to live in union with nature. Legend told that she had lived for hundreds of years amongst the Terralis, then disappeared into the forest. They believe that she is the forest itself, thriving still amongst the Terralis, and providing them with a home. The Terralis strive each moment to live in the likeness of Va'Traela, having respect and love for nature and the forest around them. This blind faith of the Terralis was so refreshing to Prinot, that he too believed immediately that the Va'Traela was the forest.

The Tale of the Terrali Nighthunters

Prinot told them of Va'Haluc. He told them that Va'Haluc was a Valazen, like Va'Traela, and how they had left the Budora together with other Valazen to protect it from afar. Va'Haluc had taken the realm of darkness and night to protected while also guarding and keeping their sleep and dreams. Va'Traela had assumed protection of the Terralis and the Forest. He told them how Va'Haluc watched over each night and watched over them from the stars.

"Why, we live in the likeness of Va'Haluc!" Kelfaine cried happily. "We protect the night from the evils that live within it and we fight to keep the sleep of our village at peace!"

This, again, delighted the Nighthunters, and they set off into the forest with a new purpose and vigor in their lives.

Prinot lead them deep into the dark forest, into an area where the silwirs became sparse, and the dense pines made passage through difficult. The Nighthunters showed no fear, but it was apparent that they were not as comfortable in this area of the forest.

They came through a clump of pine trees and came face to face with an immense black bear. The Terralis poised for action, and drew their weapons. Bleithz was the first to move, and he leapt towards the bear, with a lithe twist mid-air, and swung a sideways slice across the bear's throat. His sword met with the thick hide of the bear, and barely cut through the skin. Bleithz landed on his feet facing the bear, and for an instant they stood staring at each other, both looking slightly surprised. The bear then raised one paw and wiped it across Bleithz's chest, tearing his tunic to ribbons and slicing his chest to bleed. Bleithz groaned in pain, but did not retreat.

Instead, he screamed and ran towards the bear and began hitting him over the head with the flat side of the sword. The others followed suit, and soon all five of them were on top of the bear, nearly pinning it to the ground, beating it mercilessly with their weapons. The bear finally tired of the beating and with a loud growl, shook the elves off of his back and stood back on his hind legs. The Nighthunters tumbled to the ground and rolled and scrambled to stand, but it was too late. The bear had turned and run into the forest. The Nighthunters stood up, dispirited and humiliated and turned to face Prinot, who they thought most surely would be disappointed in their performance.

As they turned to Prinot it was their turn to be surprised. Prinot had his head down and his shoulders were shaking uncontrollably. The five black-haired, dark-clad elves curiously watched Prinot, as he stood shaking silently. Then suddenly Prinot threw his head back and laughed out loud. The Terralis jumped back quite surprised. Tears rolled down Prinot's cheeks as his laugh boomed through the quiet night forest. The jolly little Terralis were so taken aback by this large man crumbling at the mercy of his own laughter, they simply looked back and forth at each other, then back at the human who was struggling to breath between his laughs.

Soon, though, the Nighthunters began laughing and teasing each other as well, and the six of them shared a good long laugh. The stars twinkled in the night sky above them as though they too were enjoying Prinot's first good laugh in decades. If you had studied the lines on Prinot's face that night, you might believe that his laugh and smile lines were used far more than the lines that marked his worries. These Nighthunters had made him once again a happy man, and the loss of his true love, Graycliand, was no longer weighing heavily on his heart.

Prinot hunted every night after that with the Nighthunters, teaching them to hunt the larger and stronger creatures. Deeper and deeper into the dense pine forest they would go to find larger black bears. He taught them to work together to quickly attack and kill the bears. He taught Bleithz to bring his first attack across the inside of the bear's rear leg, as this area was the softest and would render the bear unable to run. He taught them to wait to attack until the bear had moved so that its weakest spot was open for attack, and taught them how to work as a team to make that happen.

The Nighthunters would show no fear, no humiliation, and no concessions as they learned to fight the rabid mountain wolves, poison grey asps and the night owls with talons like daggers. Every night was a success for them, and they would return after each night of hunting to the Prinot's hut at the edge of the forest to light a fire and retell every story of the evening. They all laughed at chattered and discussed where they would go the following night. They began to devise strategies on their own, and Prinot watched with delight. None of these five elves attacking alone would be able to defeat the foes they were finding, but together their spirituality and teamwork made them nearly invincible to everything they would encounter.

Once they ventured outside the forest and were ambushed by a pair of huge ghrillyss that were twice the size of even Prinot. They were oxen-sized creatures with movable horns that can point forwards or backwards, white fur and boar-jaws.

Surely and silently, and in complete rhythm with each other, the Nighthunters began circling the ghrillyss. Step by step, each Terrali stepping exactly in time with each other, they faced the ghrillyss and circled around them. The ghrillyss, though much larger and stronger than the elves, could not begin to comprehend the strategy the elves were using. Occasionally they would strike out at one of the Terralis, who would evade the attack and immediately get back in step with the rest of the group.

Prinot stayed back and watched as Aewanne and Chantreitta spun themselves out of the circle and into hiding, yet the ghrillyss did not miss them. The three boys continued their slow march around the ghrillyss, step by step then abruptly stopped, and ducked down. The ghrillyss blinked in surprise, but it was too late, Aewanne and Chantreitta were already in action. Aewanne shot a perfect arrow into the right arm of one of the ghrillyss. Chantreitta vaulted out from behind a rock and implanted her dagger deep into the right arm of the other. Completely surprised by the attack, the ghrillyss were helpless. Jennser threw his whip out, managing to entangle one of each of their legs and then pulled, knocking both the ghrillyss to the ground. Bleithz and Kelfaine then leapt together, each plunging their weapons through the hide of the ghrillyss and into their hearts. Prinot was amazed and confident with the Terralis progress in fighting.

Prinot would take some time every evening to tell them more about Va'Haluc. He told them all the tales he knew of Va'Haluc, and Va'Haluc's fight to keep the realms of darkness and dreams free of evil. The Nighthunters listened silently when Prinot taught them of Va'Haluc, and vowed to each other to also guard the realm of night for their people. They wanted to be just like Va'Haluc, and begged Prinot every night to tell them more. Prinot struggled to revive his knowledge of his god, and his faith came with it. Once, Prinot told them of a vision he had of Va'Haluc under a star-covered pitch-black sky, standing beside a pure white horse, bedecked in dark shadow-grey clothing. After that, they began wearing the same rich shadow-grey color as he had described Va'Haluc wearing. They even stitched in black the shimmering sword of Va'Haluc upon their tunics, above their hearts.

Prinot was also learning. He was learning to love the forest and the meadow, and appreciate the Terrali way of life, and believe in Va'Traela's blessing on the Terralis. The Nighthunters brought him a pair of suede laced boots, which he rolled down when they began their hunt, and laughed with them at the enormity of his feet inside the boots. He spoke more of their language now, and was beginning to understand the songs they sang. His favorite song, the Nighthunters prayer, had gained a new verse since he'd first heard it. One starry night he finally made them stop and teach him the prayer:

> *When the darkness of the night,*
> *devours the day,*
> *thus burgeons the realm that is ours*
> *Under the ill night sky above,*
> *We dance underneath!*
> *The stars flicker above,*
> *We shine steady below!*
> *Among the creatures of dark*
> *We stand guard*
> *For within our hearts forever*
> *burns the steady light of hope!*
>
> *For we are the Nighthunters,*
> *We are the darkness,*
> *We are the creatures,*
> *All others will fear.*
> *With the grace of Va'Traela,*
> *We are the sentinels of the forest*
> *For within our hearts forever*
> *burns the steady light of hope!*

The Tale of the Terrali Nighthunters

As he stands under his sky,
As he guards under his stars,
As he fights in his darkness,
As he shelters in his night,
As he shares his visions through dreams,
As he gives his dreams,
In Va'Haluc's realm,
For within our hearts forever
burns the steady light of hope!

They sang and laughed deep into the night. It seemed nothing could break the happiness and peace Prinot was feeling that evening. Nothing lasts forever, and that night, the peace was broken.

XI.   Reliving the nightmare

It began with a low rumble that sounded like far off thunder, and the Terralis suddenly froze, their eyes wide and their mouths open. "The Talisman!" Bleithz screamed, and they all jumped to their feet and began running into the forest. A split second behind them, Prinot jumped up, and followed them through the forest. They were running so fast, with effortless grace, and so quietly, that Prinot had a hard time keeping them within sight. The rumbling sound was getting louder and longer, and for one instant he glanced in the direction of the sound and had to stop running. He saw its source. It was true; the story of the talisman, for high above the trees was a huge storm cloud, spinning quickly. The cloud was being illuminated from below with a deep purple glow, a violet light that reminded him of something. He stood absolutely still, bewildered at the sight of the cloud and the glow, and stunned by the memory of the vivid violet. The violet the same as her eyes.

"Prinot! Come quickly!"

Jennser was shouting with fear in his voice. Prinot blinked out of his trance and ran towards Jennser's voice, drawing his sword as he ran. He caught up with the group at the base of the mountain, near the small cave that had been blocked with rocks. The faces of the Nighthunters were ashen of color and they were staring up the mountain. Prinot looked up and saw the dog-like creatures crawling down the mountain on their stout legs of ooze. From inside the cave he could hear the moaning of the creature that they had blocked in the cave. A desperate, terrifying scratching sound was coming from the rocks. It was trying to escape.

"They've come back this time! They'll attack the town!"

Bleithz made the announcement but was apparently unsure of what exact actions to take. Prinot saw fear in their faces for the first time, but none of them ran. Prinot told them to take positions; the dogs were no larger than the wolves they had hunted over and over again.

The Terralis immediately regained their stature and drew their weapons, and readied themselves for the beasts. Prinot looked back for another moment. The cloud still circled over the forest, and the violet glow was brighter than before. The dog-beasts were close now, slinking down the side of the mountain like a poison. There were only five of them in all, and he was sure that the six of them could take them easily, but he hoped that Montrealu would end it before that happened.

The dogs reached the base of the mountain and ran snarling towards the group, leaping at them. The Terralis all dodged the leaping canines and attacked them. Their weapons, just as before, were useless against the dogs. They flowed through them as though neither the dog nor the weapon knew of the other's existence. Prinot leapt behind Bleithz and swung at one of the dog's necks. The edge of his sword glowed brighter as it entered the black body of the beast. With a blood-curdling yelp, the dog was beheaded. The Terralis were backing away from the rest of the dogs in a line, trying to block them from advancing further on the village. Prinot attacked another, slicing open its abdomen and killing it immediately.

Then one barked and jumped at Kelfaine, knocking him onto his back. Kelfaine's head landed on a sharp stone with a loud crack. With a sickly whimper, his eyes rolled back into his head and he was unconscious. The dog stood on top of Kelfaine, drooling down on the unconscious boy. It slowly bared its teeth with a low rumbling growl.

The others were screaming for Kelfaine to wake up, but his body remained still under the dog as the dog lifted its head and howled. They were attempting to lure the two other dogs away from the village.

Prinot scrambled over towards Kelfaine as the dog's head lowered onto Kelfaine's throat. In the same instant, Prinot's blade touched the back of the dog's neck, the dog's teeth touched Kelfaine's throat, the glow abruptly stopped. Prinot's blade sliced through a grey wisp of smoke that was the dog. The other dogs disappeared, too. The moaning from inside the cave and the scratching stopped, yet after a silence, a soft moaning weep could be heard from behind the rocks.

The Terralis bravely regrouped but poor Kelfaine was still unconscious.

"We must get him back to the village, quickly." Said Bleithz.

Jennser and Bleithz each took Kelfaine by an arm and began walking into the forest towards where the storm had been, Kelfaine's feet dragging limp on the ground.

Prinot realized that the glow had come from their village which must have been very close by. He'd been in that part of the forest before and had seen no signs of it. Aewanne and Chantreitta lead Prinot back to his hut. They barely spoke a word to him and left him quickly. He sat up all night by himself fearing the worst for the Terralis who had no defense whatsoever against the evil beings that plagued their beautiful forest. This night, the lines of worry on his face returned.

Just as the sun was coming up the four Nighthunters, all except Kelfaine, came back to Prinot's hut. He was still sitting outside alone.

"The elders have requested that you come with us to the village" Bleithz said. He, too, looked worried, but his face was barely showing it. Lines of worry and sadness come over time, and this may well have been the first time the Terralis were truly worried.

Prinot knew that this invitation was unheard of in Tarbenlief, so he simply nodded and stood. Bleithz smiled and began walking into the forest. Prinot and the others followed quietly.

"That was the first time the beasts have been back in the ten years we have been watching over the village," Bleithz said as they walked.

"We returned to town and told our village what had happened. The people are most grateful to you"

"Our weapons are useless, yet you slew two of the dogs. Why do you believe that is?"

Bleithz seemed completely confused and frustrated.

"I believe that my weapon still holds the blessing of Va'Haluc." Prinot replied, "His blessing, like him, may aid in the smiting of creatures of the night"

Bleithz nodded as though conceding. Prinot's heart sunk seeing the Elves this dejected and broken. He followed Bleithz and the others deeper into the forest and then finally they stopped. The sun had finished it's ascent and the sky was light. Prinot looked up into the trees squinting through the sunlight seeing nothing but leaves and branches.

The Terralis cupped their hands in their mouths and began making a sound that was like birds singing. Each of them made a different sound, loud and repeating, calling up into the trees. From between the branches, between the dense leaves, suddenly five ropes dropped down. They dropped straight down to the ground but their tops disappeared up in the trees.

Bleithz held one of the ropes and motioned to Prinot to come. Aewanne, Jennser and Chantreitta began climbing the ropes quickly. Prinot grabbed hold of the rope and pulled it sharply. It was tight and strong, certainly able to hold his weight. It was the strength of his own arms that he doubted would be up to the climb.

He began climbing, hand over hand, drawing his legs up afterward, watching the elves, and following their motions. He climbed slowly. Had the situation not been so dire, he was sure that the Terralis would have found amusement in his inability to climb faster.

As he passed the lowest set of branches he looked up and still saw nothing but leaves. The Terralis had stopped just a bit ahead of him and were sitting on the branches waiting for him to catch up. He pulled himself onto a large branch and sat and rested his tired arms. The silwir trees were immense, much bigger than he imagined from the ground.

The Terralis grabbed their ropes and climbed up out of sight. Prinot took a few deep breaths and pulled himself onto his rope and began climbing again. From this deep inside the tree canopy he could neither see the ground below nor a village above. He continued to climb with the Terralis. They were patient, stopping occasionally to sit on a limb and allow him catch his breath.

Finally he saw the top of his rope tied to an enormous limb. Two other male Terralis reached down to him and pulled him up onto the limb with them. The other Nighthunters were already there, and were motioning him to a rope ladder that dangled down to them. He climbed the rope ladder through a hole and pulled himself to a standing position inside a round wooden hut built on a branch. His head touched the thatched roof above him as he stood. The hut was empty except for a wooden bench that encircled the inside of the hut. The door was a small arched frame that led out onto the huge silwir branch.

The other Terralis climbed up into the hut and headed through the doorway. Prinot ducked through the door after Bleithz and saw the Terrali village called Tarbenlief, the most breathtaking sight he had ever seen. He stood for a few moments in amazement.

Tarbenlief spanned the top of dozens of giant silwir trees, whose giant limbs crisscrossed and mixed to create a beautiful latticework of roadways and paths throughout the village. Terralis, busy with their day-to-day lives were walking, leaping and running over the limbs from hut to hut with the ease and grace he had learned to love. The village was bustling with activity, and despite the discouragement and desperation of the Nighthunters, the villagers all seemed to be peaceful and happy.

The huts spanned the limbs in all shapes and sizes. Larger huts sat nestled and anchored to the trunks of the giant silwirs. Smaller huts were built on or hung from the branches. They were interconnected by tree limbs or bridges made of rope and wood. The huts all had doors on more than one side. Some had rope ladders leading out of their roofs up to higher branches. Looking up Prinot could see the sky above the village through what looked like endless layers of huts, branches, bridges and rope ladders.

Each hut was stunning in its simplicity and grace and stood in complete harmony with the silwir trees and each other. They were framed in wood, thatched, and mortared with clay the color of a pale sunset. With the sunlight shining on the huts, they seemed to glow back with a light of their own. The Terralis had pressed dried flowers into the surface of the clay, in intricate and unique designs around the doors and windows. Silk pennants of bright colors were tied to the doorways, making each hut a work of art in true Terrali form.

Several large thatched platforms served as decks where the townsfolk would gather and chat. All through the town Prinot could hear the beautiful lilting voices of the Terralis talking and calling to each other. Their voices were accompanied by the sound of gentle breezes wafting through the treetops and the ropes creaking from the bridges and hanging huts.

The village was a feast for Prinot's tired eyes and ears. He could have stood for hours absorbing the sights, sounds and activity of the town. The Nighthunters had other plans, so Prinot followed.

Bleithz led the group from limb to limb. Prinot walked slowly and deliberately. The Terralis made it look so much easier. They would walk so quickly, without a hint of hesitation while Prinot had his long arms sticking straight out to balance himself on the branches. Prinot could have sworn he saw a hint of amusement on Bleithz's face when looked back at him once, but only for a moment.

They reached a rope ladder leading up into a large hut nestled against the trunk of one of the larger trees, and climbed inside. The room was shaded and quiet; Kelfaine was lying on a mat of woven straw underneath a tiny window. His head was wrapped in canvas and herb bandages which were soaked with blood. The room smelled strongly of pungent herbs and flowers. An older Terrali woman stood at the fire pit on other side of the room stirring and tasting a pot of stewing tea. The only sound in the room was the deep slumber breathing of Kelfaine.

"He's sleeping." She said softly, turning to smile at Prinot. She nodded to Prinot kindly and poured a cup of tea and set it next to Kelfaine.

"He cannot wake, his head is badly hurt. Our herbs cannot seem to stop the bleeding."

Prinot only understood "sleeping" and "hurt" but her face told him that Kelfaine's life was in danger, and his heart sunk. He had only spent a matter of months with the Nighthunters, but his life had been touched deeply. He had taught them as much as he could about hunting and fighting and in return they had taught him to find his spirituality and regain his faith. Even though he had taught them to fight so well, it was not enough against the very evils they were preparing for. Aewanne and Chantreitta sniffed their tears back and leaned on each other looking down at Kelfaine.

Prinot kneeled next to Kelfaine and took his hand in his own and from the very depths of his soul he prayed for Kelfaine. He prayed to Va'Traela and he prayed to Va'Haluc. He bowed his head, closed his eyes tightly and recited every prayer he had ever known. When he was finished, he continued murmuring verses from his heart just for Kelfaine. The other Nighthunters and the woman medic dropped to their knees and wept and prayed with him. Prinot begged Va'Haluc to show mercy to the boy Kelfaine and vowed his eternal servitude in exchange.

Afterwards, Prinot remained still and quiet for many moments and it seemed the entire village became silent with him. Prinot lifted his head and looked down upon Kelfaine, who was still unconscious. His deep, rhythmic breathing was the only sound in the room. Prinot watched Kelfaine, looking for some sign that his prayers had been answered, but still only the deep trancelike breathing. Aewanne touched Prinot on the shoulder and rose to her feet. Slowly they all stood. It was Bleithz that broke the silence.

"There's someone you must meet now."

He bowed to Kelfaine and started out the door. Jennser followed him with a bow; Aewanne and Chantreitta leaned down and kissed Kelfaine on the cheek.

Prinot gently laid his hand across Kelfaine's forehead, and said, "Come, lad, it's time to fight ."

They left the hut through the doorway and traveled over more limbs and bridges, passing exquisite huts of all sizes. They stopped at the doorway to a small hut that was somehow built between an upper and lower limb of a tree. Bleithz knocked quickly on the little wood-slat door and called in a greeting. From inside they heard a kind, excited greeting and the sound of shuffling feet coming to the door.

The door opened and Montrealu came through the door, his eyes glued to Prinot. Montrealu was small for even a Terrali, so Prinot towered above him. He knew immediately that this was the scholar that had read the talisman and studied Tirweul. Introductions were passed over, and Montrealu excitedly beckoned the group into the hut. Inside the hut was as splendid as the rest of the village.

They were in Montrealu's study. In the center was a large polished wooden desk, covered with scrolls and books, some stacked, some open. There were a few carved wooden chairs around the room. Each piece of furniture was beautifully designed and crafted with natural woods and other materials from the forest.

Montrealu made certain that everyone was comfortable, offering tea and biscuits, and began speaking as he served. He spoke in proper Elven, which gave the conversation all the more sense of urgency and seriousness.

"These Nighthunters think very highly of you, m'lord" he began, speaking in proper Elven "It seems they have taken quite a devotion to you."

Prinot simply nodded back to Montrealu and smiled. Montrealu continued.

"They tell me that you have taught them much about fighting, and have prepared them for their role as protectors"

Again, Prinot simply nodded.

"Milord, as you know, I've been studying the talisman that beckons the evil. I cannot learn any more than I have without endangering the village, and perhaps the lives of the Nighthunters. I am at an impasse in my studies, and yet the village is still threatened."

"The magic in the Talisman is strong and evil, but I believe that I may know more about it than can be read in the runes"

Montrealu looked at Prinot solemnly.

"I need your help to know for sure"

Prinot was somewhat confused at this request, but before he could respond, Montrealu looked to the other Terralis.

"Might we have a moment alone?" he asked them.

The four Nighthunters nodded to Montrealu and left the hut. They stood just outside, chatting quietly among themselves. Montrealu paused. Then staring at Prinot with some trepidation, he reached into his cloak and pulled out a scroll of silken parchment. As he unrolled it, Prinot saw that it was his own sketch of Graycliand.

"Gray..." He said softly, choking.

Montrealu spoke softly to Prinot.

"I'd like you to tell me everything you know about her. She may be important to the secret of the Talisman"

Prinot began slowly, he had never spoken of Graycliand to anyone, besides showing his sketches and searching for her. It was difficult to relive the emotions, but with his friends in trouble, he knew he had to help.

"I met her in Veldtanil-nar, where I lived for some time. This was over thirty years ago. I had found the elves of Veldtanil-nar to be the most spiritual of any elves I had met. They were the most welcoming to my teachings of my god and spiritualism. Even they, though, challenged my words. My faith could not be questioned then. But overtime I found myself praying with more with my head than with my heart.

"We met in the streets quite unexpectedly. She was in a hurry to get back to her work, and I was in her way. She nearly knocked me down in her rush to return to her work. She dropped a leather satchel she was carrying by its strap, the contents spilling out on the street. It had been filled with empty potion vials of all kinds, and I helped her gather them up. She was terribly upset about the accident, mumbling that she had to get to the alchemist, and I tried to calm her. Once we had put everything back together for her, she stopped and looked me in my eyes and smiled.

"She was beautiful, with dark brown hair and cool green eyes. Her smile was so sincere and pure; it melted my heart when she looked at me. I told her that the gods had seen fit for us to meet and that I was already a better man for it. This seemed to surprise her, and she blushed and thanked me. I had to convince her to let me walk with her to the alchemist.

"She made me happy from that very moment, and I became happier as we grew closer. She knew she could find me in the libraries, and she did so almost daily after that. I would look up and there she'd be, smiling at me, delivering me to happiness.

"Graycliand was different than the rest of the elves that I had met. Knowing now that she is a Terrali, I understand why. She told me that she had lived in Veldtanil-nar most of her adult life, but she was so much more emotional than the elves there. She would ask me about my life, and my faith, and she would listen, not try to argue and analyze it. She seemed completely satisfied spending hours listening to me talking and praying.

"Our love grew slowly. So interested she was in everything I did, and everything I had to say. She truly seemed to care and want to learn so much more. We began spending more time together talking and sharing our lives. We traveled outside the city to the mountains and rivers, and began spending our evenings together walking, dining, talking and laughing. I was truly in love with her, and I began to hope that we would spend our lives together.

Prinot stopped and swallowed a sip of tea. These emotions were hard to draw upon.

"She told me she had no family. She seemed willing to follow me in my travels. She completed my life, I had never been happier or more at peace then when I was with her. I believe she felt the same way."

Prinot stopped to drink more tea. Although he was talking about something that had brought him so much happiness, the lines showing on his face were the lines of worry. He sighed and took a deep breath and continued.

"She was working as an apprentice for an older Elf that was studying alchemy. She ran his errands, and aided him in his chambers during the day. In the evenings she always told me she needed to retire early so that she could be ready in the morning. Our time together was always limited by her duties to him. She asked me many times if I was interested in alchemy, and I told her, no. I was a priest, and had neither the knack nor the interest in learning elements and their magic. She told me that the Elf she worked for studied both Valazen and elemental circles of magic, but she would not tell me much more about him. She did tell me that he was old and powerful and that he was extremely dependent on her services. She seemed very devoted to him and his studies.

"The more we fell in love, the more we spoke of leaving Veldtanil-nar together. While she seemed to want to, she also seemed to be worried about leaving him almost afraid of leaving him. She wondered how he would fare without her aiding him. I tried to tell her not to torment herself over that, but that I would stay as long as she needed. It seemed the more we spoke of leaving, the more she became distressed over leaving. She began leaving me earlier and earlier every evening, and we began spending less time together. I was not concerned because our souls still connected, and our love thrived."

Prinot stopped and swallowed.

"I was selfish and my only thought was of being with her forever. I should not have pushed so hard."

"Finally, I was ready for us to begin our lives together as one. One night, after we had shared a beautiful supper outside on the lawn of a plush garden, I told her I was ready to leave Veldtanil-nar, and wished her to come with me. I asked her to marry me right then under the night stars. She wept softly and told me how much she loved me. She told me she wanted to go with me and spend her life by my side. It had grown late into the evening, much later than she normally stayed with me, yet she did not leave. She simply laid her head on my chest and wept. I thought that moment would last forever, and so would our lives together.

"Suddenly, though, she grabbed her throat, squeezed her eyes shut and seemed unable to breathe. She said, I think, 'Raenick, no!' I jumped to my feet and tried to help her, but she shook her head and pushed me away. She was holding her neck and gasping for air, and trying to make her way out the garden. I ran after her and caught up to her in the courtyard. I was able to catch her arm, and when I pulled her to me, she opened her eyes and looked at me. Her eyes...."

Prinot stopped speaking. He closed his own eyes and shook his head as if the memory was unsettling him.

"Her eyes seem to glow with an eerie shade of violet, I think, I can't be sure. It was all so sudden, and she closed her eyes again and turned away from me. I was so shocked I released her arm, and she ran away into the night."

Prinot closed his eyes tightly and hung his head.

XII. Prinot's faith

"I never heard from her again. I combed the streets of Veldtanil-nar for over a year looking for her. No one, it seemed, had ever seen her before or since her disappearance. I became depressed and self-absorbed during that year. I renounced my faith, saying that no god would take away something so dear to me.

"For the past thirty-five years I have been looking for her. Slowly though, I've lost hope, and with that the inclination to continue looking. I don't know what brought me to sketching that picture that day, but it has brought me here. Now I've found a new kind of happiness here in your forest."

He paused.

"I still don't quite understand how she can be important to your talisman.

Montrealu had been leaning back in his chair, drinking his tea, listening to Prinot carefully. He leaned forward onto his desk and set down his tea. With one slim hand, he pushed the sketch of Graycliand slowly toward Prinot and tapped it slowly with one finger.

"What is it she is wearing around her neck, m'lord?"

Prinot looked down at the sketch. He had drawn in the necklace she had worn each time he had seen her, but with not nearly the detail he had drawn the rest of the sketch. He shrugged slightly and shook his head.

"It's her necklace, a simple thin chain with a stone hanging from it. I think it had a gold symbol carved into the stone. I never really took much interest in it. The stone was… violet"

Montrealu tapped the sketch again with his finger.

"Do you know where it came from?"

Again Prinot simply shook his head slowly, staring at the sketch as though if he looked hard enough, the detail would come back to him.

"Could you draw the symbol she wore in more detail?" Montrealu asked, still tapping the sketch with his finger.

Prinot's head simply continued to shake, he remembered the necklace, but really thought very little of the symbol she wore. "I remember that it was a small, simple symbol. It was neither a symbol of the gods, nor a symbol of the stars or constellations. It was not a symbol I have seen before or since. I might recognize it if I saw it again, but I do not remember its detail, I'm sorry"

Montrealu then reached into his desk and pulled out the silver case. As he began to open it, he touched a finger to his lips indicating to Prinot to be silent. Prinot knew immediately what it was and watched intently while Montrealu pulled out the chained talisman. Again, the violet, and again his emotions flooded his mind. It was both beautiful and horrifying at the same time. The beauty of the flawless crystal, sparkling innocently, while the evil it brought to this magical village in the trees glaring from the golden runes etched on each of its eight sides.

Montrealu turned the talisman over in his hands, adjusting his spectacles on the end of his nose and squinting through them to concentrate on each side of the talisman.

"Ahh," he said finally.

He held the talisman close to Prinot, tapping one side. Prinot obliged him, looking over the etchings on the side of the talisman he was holding. They were so tiny, so delicately and perfectly etched. But the first etched symbol was indeed the symbol Graycliand wore around her neck. Prinot nodded silently tapping gently the symbol that he had seen so many times. Montrealu then turned the talisman over to another side and tapped the symbol engraved on that side. Prinot stared at it long and hard, then shook his head. Montrealu nodded.

Montrealu put the talisman back in his case, and shut it tightly.

"Yes, as I thought, the first was indeed the symbol Graycliand wore."

Prinot nodded. Montrealu continued.

"The other symbol was the symbol the Tirweul's use for Va'Nhegel."

Prinot knew what this all meant before Montrealu said anything. It was so obvious to him now; he should have known it all along. Graycliand was not the apprentice to a kind old Elf; she was his slave. He had control over her the entire time Prinot had known her. She would bid his leave so suddenly; he always thought it was that she was obeying him like a father.

"Raenick... the name she called out when she fled from me, that must be the Elf"

Montrealu nodded to Prinot. He wondered why she never told him the truth about him. Was she ashamed? Was she protecting him? He never thought to ask for he had been so in love and so happy. She had hidden her fears and secrets from him so well. He may never find out the truth.

Prinot felt more helpless now than he had ever felt about Graycliand. She had been in trouble and he wanted to help her, but the frustration of searching for years overwhelmed him, and the anger welled up inside him. His conflicting faith and emotions were overwhelming him, he felt weak and sick. His eyes started to tear up, and he just stared helplessly at Montrealu.

Montrealu slowly nodded his tiny Elven head to Prinot, and held his arm.

"Yes, that is what I thought. This poor woman in the sketch is the object of the talisman, and is your lost love."

He looked at Prinot, who was struggling, still trying to get a handle on his emotions.

"M'lord Prinot, this woman is Terrali, this is no coincidence that our town is threatened by this talisman. I believe she has come home, she is somewhere nearby, and that is why when I read any part of the runes on the talisman, the magic begins so quickly."

"The Nhegelian Channel, it's real too?" Prinot's voice shook as he spoke.

"I have always thought so. But even the Tirweul Elves speak of it as only an ancient legend. But this is the first real evidence I have found."

Montrealu looked concerned but confident.

"I have not shared that legend with our village. I'd always hoped they would not have to know. Graycliand's predicament has brought the legend close to home. We need her.

"Not only do I believe she is nearby, but I believe that the creator of this talisman, the Elf you speak of, will find us soon. The hounds that come over the mountain are not part of the talisman's magic; they are his hounds trying to find her and the talisman itself. No doubt he will not be far behind if we attempt to read the runes again."

Prinot moaned and held his head in his hands. He wanted Montrealu to read the runes immediately and summon Graycliand to him. Nothing would matter as long as he had her back. But the town would suffer such a terrible wrath if he did and they were not able to defend themselves. He blamed himself for the entire terrible situation. Had he not pushed her so hard to leave with him, and had hefocused more on her; perhaps he could have rescued her from her terrifying fate before she had returned here to bring terror on the Terralis. He continued to blame himself for the Terrali's failures, as he knew his weapon had been blessed by his mentor. He had left his studies of the magical blessings and had never attempted a blessing.

But what had become of her, and how did the talisman get taken out of the Elf's hands? Had she taken it herself? How was it buried in the meadow so long ago? And if she indeed was nearby, why had she not come out of hiding and asked the Terralis for help? There were so many questions, yet no way of answering them.

"M'lord, would you like to hear my thoughts?"

Montrealu asked softly. Prinot lifted his head and nodded to Montrealu.

"I think Graycliand wanted to be free of her slavery, and knew something of how to do it. She must have thought she could not attempt it alone, so she came here with the talisman."

Montrealu fidgeted with the silver case in his hand, running his fingers across the shiny silver.

"I believe she somehow lost this case. While she may be nearby, she may not be able to find her way to us. I am unsure why a Terrali would be lost so close to home, but perhaps she needs a guide, a beacon so to speak, to guide her here."

Montrealu continued to rub and fidget with the case.

"Now that I know for certain what the talisman is, I don't think we have much choice of what to do, m'lord. Destroying the talisman would bring certain ruin to our village, its power and magic released uncontrolled could bring upon us evils that are unthinkable. We also cannot simply close the case and forget about the beasts. Graycliand's proximity to us has most certainly gained the attention of the Elf who enslaved her. Eventually he will find her and our forest. I need not remind you how we Terralis feel about having our home discovered by a Tirweul-nar Elf and the curse of Emminda befalls us. Tarbenlief is the closest village to the edge of our forest, but there are many more. No, Prinot, our choices are few, we need Graycliand's knowledge to rid us of this curse."

Prinot stared blankly at Montrealu.

"Are you suggesting we use the talisman to summon her?"

Montrealu fixed his eyes on Prinot and nodded slowly.

"Yes, lord, I am" Montrealu replied, "but we'll need your help."

Prinot's mind was a whirlwind of hope, desperation, guilt, anger, love and hate, but Montrealu looked at him with sheer confidence. Prinot managed to set aside his doubts and focus on what he was saying.

"It will be extremely dangerous if the hounds find us before Graycliand does. The entire village will be in danger, for surely, Raenick will be right behind them. His wrath upon us will be unthinkable. You must keep the hounds from the village while I read the rune that summons her. There will be many, as I won't stop reading until she comes."

Prinot knew that he would need the help of the Nighthunters and perhaps others to fight off the hounds. One man could fight a handful of them, but he did not know how many hounds would come. If what they had seen near the mountain was any sign, there could be hundreds of them. Prinot told Montrealu that he would attempt to achieve Va'Haluc's blessing for their weapons, but that he had not prayed in so many years, he was doubtful if it his favor would be given.

Montrealu simply smiled at Prinot and said

"Your heart, m'lord, is stronger than you know. The Nighthunters believe in you completely, and you have taught them to believe in themselves. What god would not see this as a sign of eternal faith?"

Prinot drew his sword and tilted it in front of himself, gazing into the grey shimmer as though he was gazing into his own soul.

He took a deep breath and nodded to Montrealu.

"This night, in Va'Haluc's night, I shall try to commune with Va'Haluc and gain his favor and blessing for the Nighthunters."

Montrealu smiled and nodded

"I shall call a village meeting for just after dark. We'll share our plans with the townsfolk and prepare them for the coming storm."

Montrealu stood from his desk and opened a wooden chest under the window from which he pulled a small leather sack. He stood and walked to Prinot, kneeled and bowed deeply. Prinot bowed back to the tiny Terrali hierophant who looked both relieved and worried. Montrealu walked with him outside the door, where the Nighthunters had been waiting for him. Montrealu spoke quickly and softly to Bleithz and the others, telling them of the plans that were made. The Nighthunters even after what they had seen and endured, still showed only confidence and eagerness, not a touch of fear or anticipation could be seen in any of their faces. They nodded as they received the orders from the calm little Terrali elder. He gave the sack to Bleithz.

"Come, lord, follow us, Montrealu wishes you to see the forest"

Bleithz nodded to Prinot. The Nighthunters and their priest left the tiny hut of Montrealu walking over the limbs and bridges upward. It was late afternoon now, the sun was moving downward shining light through the leaves that was more orange than yellow. The clay of the huts seemed even rosier by its light.

They climbed up past four or five more levels of huts, lean-to's, bridges, and platforms, each bustling with as much activity as the lower levels. The Terralis could walk over even the tiniest limbs as though they were on flat ground, while Prinot searched for handholds the entire trip.

Looking down on the dozens of levels of the village, Prinot realized the immensity of the silwir trees upon which they were built and the city itself. The buildings and huts nearer the top of the village seemed newer, as though the trees themselves were growing to accommodate the growing Terrali villages. The entire forest seemed to grow and live simply to house the Terrali people, it did not escape Prinot why they wanted to keep it to themselves and minimize the visitors.

They were now at the top of the village. Bleithz pointed at a rope ladder that wound up the trunk of the tree from the branch they were standing. Prinot looked up and followed the rope with his eyes to a tiny hut, perfectly round with a wooden balcony wrapping around it. Bleithz climbed up first, followed by Aewanne and Chantreitta. Jennser indicated for Prinot to climb up next. Prinot climbed the tiny rope ladder that creaked with his weight as he stepped on each rung. He climbed through the small hole in the bottom of the hut, and walked out onto the thin balcony with the others.

He felt higher than he'd ever felt on any mountain he had ever climbed before. The sun was setting in the west, shining its orange-drenched rays on the tops of the trees. Even from this height, the forest seemed to reach forever into the east. To the west, he could see the Mountains, and even the meadow he had come across to the forest. The meadow seemed a miniature garden from this high, but he could see the plush green grass and flowers from his perch. To the east he could see nothing but lush treetops as far as he could see. So thick a forest with no end it seemed. It looked as though new growth nudged its way into life between trees, nudging the east edge of the forest over the edge of Budora. Bleithz stood next to Prinot and let him take in the immense view.

"That is Gymockdon over there"

Bleithz said, and pointed to an area in the trees that seemed sparse. From the sack he pulled an iron telescope and gave it to Prinot. Prinot extended the instrument and held it to his eye. With it, he could see that Gymockdon was another Terrali village, at least 20 miles away, but even larger than Tarbenlief. From the top of its highest tree stood another hut like the one in which they were standing. Bleithz pointed slightly southeast of their tower.

"And that is Ytmerrgian, and over there," he said pointing due northeast "is Kussajaken. There are many more villages farther into the forest, those are the closest. They are our sister villages, I'm to tell them of our plight, they will send messages to the other villages."

Bleithz removed two bundles of silk from his pack, and untied the cinch string around them. Inside each of them was a handful of bright-colored dust, one green and one yellow. He poured some of the dust onto an iron disk that sat on the edge of the balcony into two piles. He lit both of them with a match, and immediately thick green and yellow smoke billowed from the dust piles. The smoke rose high into the sky, barely mixing, but swirling slowly around each other. Bleithz pulled a bugle from the sack and began blowing long, low tones into the late afternoon sky. The other Nighthunters scanned the top of the forest carefully, searching for something. Moments later, streams of green smoke rose up from the other three towns and similar bugle calls could be heard faintly from the distance. Bleithz lowered his bugle and smiled.

"They will come to join us tonight"

The sun continued to set. Prinot had been so enthralled with standing higher than the forest and appreciating how very vast and beautiful the true Terrali way of life was, that he had, for a moment, forgotten of the pain and horror that awaited them.

After the sun set the villagers gathered at the largest meeting platform in the village. Prinot sat at one edge flanked by the four Nighthunters, the elders in the middle around a fire. Terrali villagers filled every inch of the platform, spilling over onto the balconies of every nearby hut, sitting over the branches, and on the rope slung bridges overhead. They all sat silently, waiting word from the elders on the state of the talisman.

Bleithz leaned close to Prinot and whispered to him,

"Those that you see on that end of the platform are from the neighboring villages. Gymockdon has sent over fifty delegates, Ytmerrgian sent thirty-three, and Kussajaken sent forty-eight. They have come to help. Others will come too, our force will hundreds"

Montrealu spoke. He told the Terralis everything with as much confidence as when he had spoken to Prinot. The villagers were frightened, Montrealu did not exaggerate their fear of the dark elves and Tirweul-nar and they were terrified at the thought of the Elf finding their home. They seemed content that Montrealu and the elders had made the proper decision, and no one questioned their wisdom.

After the Montrealu had spoken, he waved Prinot to come to the center of the platform.

"This man has lead and trained our Nighthunters into noble warriors. He has agreed to aid us and lead the fighting that most certainly will accompany the summoning of Graycliand."

The Nighthunters gathered near the fire with Prinot and Montrealu.

Prinot spoke to the crowd with feigned confidence.

"First we must ready your weapons to fight the beasts that threaten your forest."

Prinot drew his sword from its sheath and held it straight up before his face. The fire had died somewhat, but the small flames jumping reflected in the grey shimmer of his sword. He glanced doubtfully at Montrealu, who simply nodded at him.

"Nighthunters, lay down your weapons."

One by one, they put their weapons in a small pile near the fire. Bleithz's broadsword, then Chantreitta's sword, Aewanne's bow and quiver, Jennser's morning star and whip all lay near the fire, black as night.

Prinot kneeled before the pile of black weapons and held his sword high over his head with both hands. He gazed up into the sky, which was entirely blanketed with stars. With an eloquent swing of his weapon over his head he prayed.

"Lord Va'Haluc, my strength and glory
We pray that you come to us now,
For we seek thy blessing
To combat the evil that threatens these people
You lead us into the blackness of night
'Tis with your strength that we have the power to fight
We pray that you will aid us in our quest
To destroy absolutely the black curse
That has befallen this village."

He held his weapon perfectly still, staring up into the stars, looking for some sign of magic, some sign of blessing. Nothing came. The four Nighthunters and all the onlooking Terralis stared up into the sky wideeyed with him. They did not know what they were looking for, but they sought the skies nonetheless.

Prinot closed his eyes tightly again, and repeated the prayer, holding his own weapon so tightly his hands were numb. The Nighthunters got on their knees and prayed, too. Still nothing happened. Prinot opened his eyes slowly and looked at the helpless pile of weapons that lay in front of him. He allowed his arms to fall and looked helplessly at Montrealu, who looked back at him with calm eyes.

"I don't know..." Prinot started to say. He was interrupted by a weak voice coming from behind him.

"Perhaps," the voice said, "it is because one of the weapons to be blessed is missing."

Prinot and the Nighthunters turned to see Kelfaine walking towards them, pale and being held up by the medic that was caring for him. His head was still wrapped, but the bandages were dry. He looked terribly weak, but he was smiling, and he was waving his dagger in weak floppy "Z's" while he hobbled slowly over the limbs to the platform.

The Tale of the Terrali Nighthunters

The Nighthunters all squealed in delight, screaming his name and ran to meet him. They were surrounding him, crying and laughing, helping him down to the platform where Prinot was standing, smiling at the brave group of Nighthunters. Prinot took Kelfaine's small forearm into his own, and held it with both hands.

"You look well, Kelfaine, I am humbled by your strength. Your inner strength has brought you to you feet." Prinot said to him

"No, Father, it was you! You came to me in my dream, my dark, dark dream"

Kelfaine said, his voice still raspy and weak. Prinot lead him to the center of the platform and let him sit and catch his breath. He sat next to him and held his arm, listening intently to Kelfaine recount his dream.

"I could not wake up, and the night was so dark and cold. I thought I was to be in darkness forever. Then, I heard you praying. I tried to come to you, but I could not move. I could not lift my head or open my eyes to see you and you sounded so far away. You were praying louder and louder, and the louder you prayed, the harder I tried to get to you. I was able to get to my knees, but I knew not the way.

"Then, a man, no not exactly a man, not a man like you, but not an Elf either, a person. He was dressed in shadow-grey clothing and rode up on a brilliant white horse. He had a sword that glowed like your own and he pulled me up onto his saddle and said 'come lad, it's time to fight'."

Prinot stared at Kelfaine remembering his last words to him as he left his hospital bed. Kelfaine continued.

"We rode together in the night forever. I could still hear you praying. We rode for many nights it seemed. It was so dark and I was afraid. The man told me that darkness was his. Then I saw you standing alone, all alone. You seemed so helpless and alone, and we rode for so long. Finally we were near you, and I was walking again. You reached out to me and I reached out for you. You said, 'Come Kelfaine, we need you.' When our hands touched, I awoke."

Prinot had tears in his eyes, as he and the other Nighhunters took their seats next to Kelfaine, near the fire, and the pile of black weapons beside it. The dream! Could his prayers for Kelfaine have been heard? His prayers by his bedside were the first in so long that he had felt so strongly. If his prayers were heard for Kelfaine's life, then surely, they would be heard here. Kelfaine put his dagger on the pile, and kneeled before it. The other Terralis knelt next to him and they all clasped hands around the pile.

Prinot again raised his sword over his head and repeated the prayer. Louder than before, and coming from his heart, he prayed again for the blessing of Va'Haluc. He bowed his head, squeezed his eyes shut, and rocked and prayed. His voice became louder and more hollow. It echoed across the trees as he prayed.

Slowly at first, hardly noticeable, the sky grew darker. The Nighthunters looked up in the sky and saw that the stars were disappearing one by one and the sky was becoming pitch black. Tiny gasps could be heard throughout the crowd.

Prinot continued to chant, rocking back and forth, holding his sword tightly in both hands over his head. The fired died suddenly as well and they were enveloped in total darkness. The Terralis, slightly afraid but silent, stared up into the sky while he chanted.

Prinot seemed to be in a trance now, chanting softly and slowly. Then suddenly, two dim stars pierced through the darkness washing everything in a pale, silvery glow. The Terralis were barely able to breath when they realized that the stars were the image of a pair of dark grey almond eyes that seem to tug at their very soul with their hypnotic, haunting gaze.

Prinot stopped chanting, slowly lifted his head and opened his heavy eyes. The whites of his eyes were now gone, replaced by the same haunting grey as the two stars that loomed above. The edge of his sword was now alit with a white fire of its own.

He held his sword tightly and lowered it slowly down towards the black weapons lying in a pile. The white fire arced from his sword down to the weapons on the pile, engulfing the pile.

Montrealu called in Terrali to the villagers and visitors and then many of them drew weapons and threw them onto the pile. The fire flared with the addition of each one, engulfing them all in its flames. The white arc from Prinot's sword continued to feed the fire as more weapons were thrown down from the Terralis perches above the platform. Dozens of weapons fell into the white fire, then hundreds, each representing a new volunteer to help guard the village.

Prinot suddenly came to his senses, and let go of his own sword, letting it land on the pile. An enormous, blinding white ball of flame exploded from the weapons and shot towards the sky. The Terralis and Prinot shielded their eyes with their arms as the flame disappeared into the night sky. Slowly they all looked up into the sky, which was once again covered with stars. Their weapons, however, now all had the shimmer of grey.

The silence afterward seemed an eternity. Prinot opened his eyes, the whites returned to normal, and gazed at the pile of glowing weapons. He wept openly, smiling through his tears. He looked at each of the Nighthunters, humbled and flattered, and whispered a quiet "thank you" to each of them in Terrali.

He took Kelfaine's hand into both of his own and said "Thank you, lad, thank you" then looked up into the heavens and whispered a quiet prayer, thanking Va'Haluc himself for watching over the night.

Then he stood, and seemed to stand taller than before, and said "Come now, we have work to do"

XIII. Raenick

The next few weeks were spent in preparation. Kelfaine's health continued to improve and respond to the herbs. It was only a matter of days before he was back in action with the Nighthunters. The new volunteers joined the Nighthunters in their nocturnal lives, in training for the battle. They worked hard, hunting the forest creatures and practicing maneuvers. Prinot assigned the five Nighthunters as block leaders, each with a following of thirty or so volunteers. They spent each night competing, drilling and fighting. Each night ended around a fire near Prinot's hut near the edge of the forest, singing and praying. The volunteers began wearing dark clothes, and each stitched an emblem of the sword in grey silk thread over their hearts. The five Nightunters became exemplary leaders of their blocks, in bravery, leadership and strength.

Prinot had complete faith once again in himself, in Va'Haluc, and even more in these determined Terrali Nighthunters. He too stitched a silver sword over his heart, and above it, he stitched the symbol that Graycliand wore about her neck. He worked harder than anyone did at preparing for battle. He spent the days sketching stalking maneuvers; line drills and combat tactics which they would practice in the nights.

Montrealu had also been preparing for the night. He spent every evening silently studying the talisman, memorizing each symbol etched on the side with Graycliand's symbol. He wanted to recite the summoning perfectly, lest more danger fall upon the village.

They were all ready twenty-three days after the village gathering, and it was time for the summoning. The villagers were told to stay in the village, in their huts, while Montrealu performed the summoning. Since they did not know where Graycliand was, or if she would be able to find the village, Montrealu came to the edge of the forest, near Prinot's hut to read the runes.

They sat in a circle and clasped hands and prayed together. Prinot lead the prayer to Va'Haluc, and they all recited the Nighthunters Prayer together. They then stood and formed a circle around Montrealu, facing outward, weapons and shields drawn and ready. Montrealu shakily opened the case and removed the Talisman. He muttered a quick prayer to Va'Traela, then began reading the runes.

His voice was strong as he chanted the writings of the talisman in the Tirweul tongue. Even the tone of the chant sounded sinister and foreboding. It wasn't long before the storm cloud formed over their heads. The Terralis looked up into the sky, questioning, but without fear. The talisman began to glow the eerie violet that had plagued the village before, glowing brighter and brighter in the hands of Montrealu. Montrealu's voice shook in fear, yet he kept reading. From deep inside the forest the moaning began. Low at first, but as the glow and the storm rose so did the pounding sound of the creature from inside the cave.

"The creature!" Prinot called out over wind of the storm "Bleithz, you are with me! Chantreitta, stay back and protect Montrealu! Awaenne, Jennser and Kelfaine, position yourselves between here and the cave. Do not let the hounds pass! Do just as we have practiced, for you are the owners of the night. Va'Haluc will be with you!"

Prinot called out the orders and they were followed immediately. Prinot, Bleithz and his block ran through the forest to the mouth of the cave. The hounds had almost beaten them there, for they were most the way down the mountain. The moaning was deafening from inside the blocked cave, and again the scratching and beating of the rocks could be heard. The hounds arrived, at least twenty of them, the first lunging at Prinot straight from the bottom of the mountain. Prinot swung his weapon around and connected with the hound at the base of his neck. It was quickly killed and lay sprawled on the rocks.

He looked down the base of the mountain, hounds were landing from here back to the hut, he could tell that all the troops were engaged with the hounds. There were hundreds of them, stalking low to the ground, approaching the line of Terralis. Bleithz and his eight companions were fighting well; taking on the hounds that had come off the mountain near the cave. The scratching and beating from inside the cave turned into pounding, so strong the rocks began to loosen and fall from the mouth of the cave.

All across the edge of the forest, from the hut to the cave, the Terralis were fighting the hounds. Their black weapons raced through the air with grace and precision, taking out the hounds one by one. But for every hound that was killed, another two started down the mountain. Hours passed, the Terralis fought gallantly, but it appeared there was no end to the oozing black hounds, and no word that Graycliand had appeared. Prinot ordered the injured Terralis into the forest for cover and safety.

At the hut, Montrealu sat within the circle of Chantreitta's group, still safe, still reading. They had killed off the first wave of hounds from the mountain, but he could see another coming. Graycliand needed to make her appearance quickly; the second wave seemed larger than the first. Where could she be? The storm was getting worse; the wind was making it difficult to stand their ground against the hounds. The glow from the Talisman became brighter and brighter suddenly, almost blinding.

The hounds were coming faster now, but someone was with them. The shape was Elven, dressed in silver and purple, wearing a cloak that billowed in the wind of the storm. He was walking, but somehow closing in on them faster than a walk should take a man as though he was riding the wind of the storm. He was walking with his pack of dogs straight towards Montrealu and the tiny group of Terralis left to guard the talisman. Chantreitta screamed out to one of her group to run, warn the others. The Tirweul Elf had come!

Near the cave, Bleithz, Prinot and company were fighting off the hounds as fast as they could come. The black creature had punched a hole in the rock wall that blocked it in. It was reaching out, pushing away rocks one at a time slowly breaking out of the cave prison. The Terrali messenger arrived and told them of the news of the Elf.

"No!" Prinot shouted back, but he knew it was true. "Bleithz, we must return to the hut! Leave the beast, we are in great danger!"

Raenick was halfway across the meadow and coming faster towards the hut. His feet seemed to glide over the grass underfoot in long slow strides, as though not even touching. His head was lowered; his stare upon the source of the glow, his enormous cloak blew behind him in the wind of the storm. In the blink of an eye he was standing over Montrealu, his mouth turned up in a wry grin, but his eyes were dark and angry. He was neat and calm, tall and straight. Not anything like the gnarled man he was when he lost possession of Graycliand. The channel had made him well and strong.

"Raenick…" Montrealu whispered.

"Ah, how very perceptive of you" The dark Elf smiled and held out his hand. His fingers were long and dark, his nails thick and black.

"I believe you have something of mine."

His smile was as crooked as his heart, as he stared at Montrealu. His eyes were black and smooth as glass, with not a trace of whites that could be seen.

"What would make a simple Terrali like you want to summon my demon, dear man?"

The yelp of a dying hound interrupted Raenick; he turned suddenly to see that Chantreitta had killed one of his hounds. He raised up his hand, flat side to Chantreitta and uttered a single word in Nhegelian. Streams of black surged from the ground and soared towards her. As though he had pushed her with unthinkable force she flew backward over ten feet into the trunk of a tree. She slumped down to the ground unconscious.

"Do not touch my servants!"

Raenick roared at her, then turned back to Montrealu, and again held out his dark hand.

"The talisman, Terrali, hand it to me now!"

His voice boomed coldly into the night.

The Tale of the Terrali Nighthunters

Montrealu clenched the talisman in his fist and stood.

"Find refuge in the forest, children, go now!"

The Terralis obeyed immediately and disappeared into the forest. He turned to run into the forest himself, but Raenick lifted his hand towards him sending another surge black essence of magic at Montrealu, it wrapped around his shin tearing his leg off at the knee. Montrealu screamed as he fell to the ground, and tried to crawl into the forest, still clutching the talisman.

In a second, Raenick was standing over the crippled Elf, his billowing cloak once again settling on his shoulders. He reached down and wrenched the talisman out of Montrealu's hand, laughing softly under his breath.

He raised his hand once again towards Montrealu. But before he could say a word, he was impaled from behind with an arrow in his shoulder. Outraged, he pulled the silver-tipped arrow out of his bleeding arm and turned to look in the direction from where it had come. He saw nothing but forest. His eyes scanned the entire area, but found nothing. He gestured to his hounds to seek and find his attacker. They obeyed at once.

He turned once again to face Montrealu but he was gone. The unconscious Chantreitta was gone as well. He stood alone at the edge of the forest, talisman in hand. He chuckled to himself, then hung the chain around his neck, lifted the talisman, and gazed deep inside.

Inside the canopy of the forest, in a small clearing, the Nighthunters had regrouped. The dogs were closing in on their location, they could hear them howling, but the dense forest was shielding them for now. They had been successful in sneaking quietly and distracting Raenick long enough to get Montrealu, Chantreitta, and the other injured to safety. Chantreitta had awoken, but was still too weak to fight. The remaining Nighthunters were tired and frightened. The hounds had been relentless. The injured reduced the force to half their original contingency. They were tired and they were losing. Raenick had the talisman, Graycliand had not returned, and the village was almost certainly doomed.

"Raenick must be destroyed, we must retrieve the talisman! Chantreitta, keep watch over this area. Be sure the injured are tended to."

Prinot placed his right hand over his heart, and lead the others through the forest towards the hut and Raenick.

When they arrived, Raenick was alone. He appeared to be in a trance, staring straight ahead, muttering softly and wearing the talisman. It was glowing brightly, illuminating his face with an eerie shade of purple. Prinot strode towards him and drew his weapon. He stepped slowly and quietly, watching Raenick cautiously, watching for movement. The Nighthunters followed, spreading out slightly staying absolutely silent.

They were still quite a distance away when Raenick's eyes fluttered only slightly and a hint of a smile touched his mouth. Suddenly his arms flew up and he faced Prinot and stared at him.

"Prinot! So now it all makes sense!"

He threw his head back and laughed.

"You've come to take her back, you fool!"

Raenick clenched his fists in the air, and the hounds came in from the forest and from the mountain. The Nighthunters jumped into battle immediately, and with fantastic speed and precision, killed them as they came. Raenick stood behind the fray, pacing back and forth, his dark eyes searching into the forest.

Then the black oozing beast came out of the forest. Slowly, arms outstretched, emitting the spine-crawling moan they had heard from inside the caves. Its clothing was in tatters still clung to its back. Bleithz and Jennser together turned to the beast. They circled it, just as they had done the ghrillys, blocking its path to the rest of the Terralis.

"Destroy it!" Prinot yelled with his eyes still focused on Raenick.

"Yes! Destroy it!"

Raenick cried from behind the lines of hounds, and he laughed maniacally at the irony. Then he lowered his voice, lowered his head, fixed his eyes on Prinot and between his clenched teeth he graveled, "It's perfect."

Bleithz and Jennser began their attack on the beast, just as Prinot had taught them. First Jennser slashed at its hands, and it swung its long black arms out at him, knocking him down. Bleithz used the moment to leap forth and nearly removed its thick sticky leg, sending it slowly to the ground, black ooze dripping out of the stump. Jennser stood and was ready to deliver the killing blow, but to their surprise, the beast's leg healed itself out of the black slime and it was standing again. They continued their maneuvers against the beast, over and over, weakening it slowly.

Meanwhile, Prinot tried to cross the line of hounds to Raenick, yet they blocked his path. When one was slain, another came in his place. He signaled to Kelfaine, and he and two others jumped over to Prinot and covered the hounds around him, allowing him to pass through to Raenick.

He took Raenick by surprise, and his first blow was powerful, swung downward from over his head into Raenick's hip. Raenick howled and shut his eyes, and fell to the ground. Prinot spun full around, recovering, and then immediately swung for Raenick's neck. Raenick managed to roll out from underneath him, and Prinot struck the forest floor with his blade.

Raenick rolled to his back and lifted his hand to Prinot, his essence hitting him in the chest, knocking him backwards, head over heels. Prinot landed heavily on his face in on the forest floor. His chest ached with coldness, and he was bleeding from a gaping wound.

He looked out at the Nighthunters. They were still fighting off hound after hound. They were winning, but they were getting worn down and making mistakes. He had to end this now. Graycliand was, for whatever reason, unable to answer the summons. That part was certain. Bleithz and Jennser were getting beaten to a pulp by the beast, yet they still persevered, hacking into its black ooze again and again.

He managed to pull himself to his feet, and renewed his grip on his sword with both hands. He turned to Raenick who was on one side, struggling to rise to his knees. Prinot was on him again in an instant, slinging his weapon clean through Raenick's left arm, which dropped to the ground beside him. Raenick's eyes widened in pain, revealing their whites, making him look much less sinister and fearsome. He looked simply wretched. He rolled onto his back, bleeding and beaten.

Suddenly, Bleithz began screaming hysterically.

"Prinot! Father! Aauuughh!" The beast had grasped him with one of its black appendages around his shoulders and was holding him close to its body. Jennser was screaming for Prinot, too, both of them seemed completely hysterical.

"Jennser! Help him! Destroy the beast!"

Prinot called out to them as he walked over to Raenick's bleeding body and stood over him, ready to kill the man who had ruined his life so many years ago. Raenick looked up at him with cold hatred. He muttered a few words, guttural and deep, bringing his one hand to his chest and clenched his fist suddenly. Immediately six black hounds, larger than the others, surrounded Prinot.. Prinot began fighting them, and though they were no match for his strength, they kept him from killing Raenick.

"Prinot!" Bleithz screamed "The beast has the symbol of Graycliand!"

Prinot stopped fighting in horror looking over at the Bleithz and the beast. He was struggling with something at the beast's neck, a chain. Though he could not see the chain and its details he suddenly knew Bleithz was right. He looked over at Raenick who was lying on his back, laughing.

"Yes, priest, it is her. Your true love that left you for me so many years ago"

A hound jumped at Prinot's throat, and he barely ducked out of the way, following it with a sword to the dog's back, slicing it in half. Raenick laughed choking on his injuries.

"It seems she has a curse upon her." He coughed from his back, causing blood to spurt into his mouth, and flow out the corners.

"Do destroy her for me. She betrayed me."

Prinot and the Nighthunters were still surrounded by hounds, they had not a moment to stop and think. Raenick was still able to mutter magical phrases and summon more hounds, which were larger and more powerful every time. If Prinot stopped fighting for a second, they would encircle him and attack, so he kept fighting.

The beast that was Graycliand still had Bleithz in its arms, squeezing him into her chest, nearly suffocating him, and Jennser was still being beaten by its appendages. Awaenne, Kelfaine and the other Nighthunters were fighting the hounds weakly. Prinot could tell they were getting worn down.

Prinot had no time to think, no time to consider minutiae, no time to plan; yet he acted in an instant. He kneeled down right there in the center of the fray. He had heard that curses could be removed, and though he did not believe he would have the power of concentration or the gift of divine intervention, he knew he had to try.

The hounds were on him immediately, biting and clawing at him, yet he did not fight. He lay down his sword before him, removed his tunic from his bleeding chest and laid it down in front of him. He lowered his head and concentrated on the symbol of Graycliand he had stitched onto the tunic. He took a few deep breaths, clenched his fists and raised them over his head and prayed.

Va'Haluc, lord of the night,
Protector of the realm of darkness and dreams
I beseech thee...

A hound leapt at him, his powerful jaw connecting with Prinot's head, knocking him down. He was bleeding from his temple, but he never moved his eyes from the symbol. He returned to a kneel and continued praying.

Give me thy guidance, lord
Help me deliver this creature from its evil curse
And protect ...

Another hound snarled and hurdled at his face, tearing his face open. The Terralis, still fighting the hounds around themselves, were screaming at him to please stop and fight, to save himself, but he continued to pray.

And protect these good people
From the evils outside their forest.

A hound raked its long black claws through Prinot's neck, and blood streamed out down his chest. Prinot put one hand over the wound and kept praying. Raenick was summoning the hounds more slowly now, but the elves were barely able to keep up.

> *These people, Graycliand and all the Terralis,*
> *Delivered me back to you,*
> *Deliver them to safety*
> *Remove her curse*
> *I beg of you, Lord.*

Three hounds were on top of Prinot now. One had a grip on his upper arm, tearing at it. The others were clawing and biting at his chest, back and neck. His voice was nearly gone.

Then from the forest came Chantreitta leading the rest of the injured Terralis. They saw the battle and the desperation on the faces of the fighting Nighthunters and jumped back into battle.

"He's dying!" cried Kelfaine "Fend off the dogs!"

He ran over next to Prinot and kneeled with him. He clasped Prinot's bloody hand and said "Pray, now, Father, if you must."

Prinot's face was too bloodied to see Kelfaine clearly, but he heard and felt him, and began chanting prayers to Va'Haluc.

Chantreitta and Aewanne immediately took on the hounds that surrounded Prinot. They managed to keep them from attacking Prinot any further as he prayed deeply and quietly, focusing on the symbol in front of him. The other Terralis, with a flood of energy, began fighting with regenerated vehemence. They worked together again, taking on two and three hounds at a time. Finally they were able to kill more than Raenick could release.

Then, abruptly, it was as though time stood still. The hounds stopped moving, and whimpered softly. The Terralis stopped fighting and looked toward Prinot. The beast froze entirely, dropping its arms and letting Bleithz drop to the forest floor. Everything stopped, even the sounds of the forest, everything except Prinot's quiet praying.

The Tale of the Terrali Nighthunters

A white light slowly dropped down from the sky, piercing through the storm cloud overhead, and bathing Prinot inside. His bloody form was rocking and praying in the blinding light.

Then he too stopped and sat up straight in the light that bathed him. He lifted a bloody arm and pointed across to the black beast.

Another white light blazed down through the sky and bathed the beast inside, then glowed so brightly, nothing could be seen but the two baths of light.

Prinot collapsed in a bloody heap on the ground next to Kelfaine, as the white light dimmed around him. It continued shining and swirling in a pool around the beast. It was bright and filled with tiny stars that swirled around the beast, higher and higher.

The bright light stopped spinning and seemed to fall gently and silently to the ground. Graycliand stepped out of the light. She stood for a few moments gazing at the battleground around her. She blinked her eyes and looked about her as if waking from a long nightmare-filled sleep. Then her eyes fixed on Prinot. A short gasp escaped her, and she held her hand to her mouth. Tears filled her eyes, and she fell to her knees.

"No! Prinot, No!"

The sound of her voice awoke the Terralis and hounds from their stillness. Once again the sound of battle filled the air as the fighting began again. Graycliand sat gazing around her with her hand to her mouth as she took in the scene around her. She looked at Raenick laying near death on the ground. She looked at the Nighthunters around her. She gazed at the starless sky and then at the forest.

Around her the battle continued and Kelfaine still kneeled beside the broken Prinot on the ground. Her face remained calm as she seemed to take in the past quarter century over only a few moments. Then Graycliand stood quietly and walked past it all to Prinot, and picked up his black sword.

"I will end this, my love"

She walked slowly to Raenick, who lay near death on the forest floor.

"Graycliand" he said, "You must save me, my slave."

He held the talisman in his hand, but the light and the glow were gone. She merely shook her head and raised her palm to the sky and clenched her fist. Vines sprung from the ground and lashed Raenick to the floor. She held Prinot's weapon in both hands high over her head, point facing downward. With a will that was finally all her own, she plunged the sword through his heart.

The hounds and the storm disappeared instantly and the forest grew quiet. The sky was starless and inky black. Raenick was finally gone, every bit of him.

The silence did not last long as the relief of the end of battle turned to the horror of Prinot's body laying still on the ground. The Nighthunters including Graycliand screamed and ran to Prinot. Graycliand clasped his hand and wept over him.

"Prinot, dear Prinot, can you hear me?" Prinot nodded his head weakly and squeezed her hand. They were all weeping and sobbing around him. He was so terribly injured; there was simply no hope.

"Prinot, I am finally free, I'll stay by your side now forever" she sobbed, "you have freed me, nothing can separate us now."

She fell apart, collapsing over his body in huge sobs.

"Graycliand…." Prinot said in barely a whisper, laboring over every word. His mouth opened a few times as he struggled to say something, but it was proving too difficult. Finally, he managed to whisper only few more words.

"Within my heart forever burns the steady light of hope. For Terrali. For the Nighthunters. For you, my love."

He squeezed her hand a final time, and there, at the edge of the Terrali forest, in Va'Haluc's realm of night, Prinot's hand went limp.

The Terrali Nighthunters cried and prayed, and not one of them noticed that in the otherwise starless sky shone a single bright star.

XIV. Epilogue

The story told here is only the beginning of the Nighthunters. After Prinot's death, they continued to grow and thrive over many years. Graycliand herself dyed her hair black, and donned the shadow-grey clothing as the rest of them and lived out her long life as a Nighthunter. It has been told that she traveled to Prinot's home of Hallardstin to become a priestess of Va'Haluc under the tutelage of Wittig himself. Even the one-legged Montrealu was said to have spent many of his nights on the forest floor singing and praying with the Nighthunters.

Legends tell that the number of Nighthunters grew, and continues to grow this very day. They still fancy themselves to be Va'Haluc-like in the nights of the forest, protecting the villages from intruders of the forest, though through the constant vigil of De'Heatah and Goharo, there are very few intruders. The Terrali's existence remains a legend.

Though it should be told that exactly two days after Raenick's death, a very confused and disoriented Groheil awoke on the floor of his home, very alone, with his pulse raging through his head.

And if you travel east of the Elven City-States and find a forest that is more lush and overgrown than most with a canopy of leaves that blocks your view of the sky, rest assured that it is protected by the Terrali Nighthunters. And if you ever set foot inside these forests, be forewarned, you may never leave.

Appendix I: Budorans

Primal Gods

The Emminent mother and her two sons:

Coveal, son of the Emminent Mother, bringer of darkness

Mindal, son of the Emminent Mother, bringer of light

Prieran beasts

Rodal Woodlike

Flotal Waterlike

Atmal Airlike

Gemal Rocklike

Valazen gods

Va'Lator, Leader of the Valazen and claimed the throne of King of the Gods. Loyal to the Eminent Mother, He proclaimed that the Eminent Mother would return and wish her treasure returned to state that would regard its original beauty along with a memory of her deceased sons. He declared that it should be the surviving Valazen's responsibility to tend to its restoration. He commanded the other Valazen to find ways of restoring Budora in both light and darkness. While all the Valazen respected Va'Lator Those Valazen that were once loyal to Mindal assumed the errand of Light, while those once loyal to mad Coveal assumed the errand of Darkness.

Va'Meogrim, daughter of Va'Decheiu, and artist of life, also loyal to the Eminent Mother. She constructed all forms of life on Budora. From Human to earthworm, she had the sketchpad of life, and blew within them the breath of the Eminent Mother. Her breath is present at every birth of every creature on Budora, without it no creature would open its eyes and breath.

Va'Thinoa and Va'Feligius, twin brothers of Va'Meogrim. Va'Thinoa pledged his allegiance to Mindal, the light. He is the god of intellect and logic. He masters that which cannot be argued. His form is of a golden owl, with crimson eyes. Va'Feligius represents all that defies logic. He is our primal emotions and needs, and follows our hearts without our minds. In the frenzy of light and darkness, he chose darkness but in the chaos of his mind could never pledge allegiance to Coveal. His form is that of a black dove.

Va'Maratt, god of the sky and sun. Devout to the Eminent Mother, he treasured the light that was always present with Mindal. After Mindal was punished and the Eminent Mother left the Budora to the Valazen, Va'Maratt pledged his undying allegiance to Va'Lator to guard the sun, light, and sky. He is the keeper of faith, and deliverer of hope. It is his faith in the ultimate return of the Eminent Mother that inspired the rest of the Mindali Valazen to conceive the beauty of life on Budora. It is Va'Maratt that can still communicate with Mindal, the sun, and urges him to shine each day on Budora, and even when conceding the sky each night to Coveal, to do it in a splendor of colored sky, and to return with the same radiant splendor each morning.

Va'Traela, daughter of Va'Maratt, is the Goddess of the Garden. She is the follower of light and the sun and among the ruins of the Great Rodal she urged Va'Meogrim to help her create life. She is the Goddess of the Forest and Meadows, and Va'Meogrim has endowed her with the breath of life. Her form is a tiny winged humanoid.

Va'Decheiu, God of Life from Death. Father of Va'Meogrim, immensely loyal to Coveal. It is he that takes the final breath from all life on Budora, opens its eyes wide and takes its soul into the depths of darkness. From there Va'Decheiu creates new life from death. Only the prayer of Va'Meogrim prior to the last breath can save a soul from the curse of Va'Decheius, as he scours the world in search of every last breath. His form is humanoid, aged and dark. His eyes are black as onyx with no whites. His cheeks are drawn and gaunt.

Va'Nhegel, King of Darkness and Chaos. Va'Decheiu's supreme malice is only surpassed by the malevolence of Va'Nhegel. He was Coveal's favorite Valazen, and prizes his place in Coveal's heart. He believes Budora and its lifeforms to be his own personal playground, to be teased and toyed and hurt. In his dark mind, lifeforms can be smothered as easily as created. Darkness is his playground and it is his breath that can take a soul into Va'Decheiu's darkness. Va'Nhegel is God of Darkness and Death His form is ethereal darkness, like that of Coveal. He surrounds us in night and sadness and is powerless in light and happiness. His form is humanoid in shape, but is formed of black smoke...

Va'Haluc, defender of the light is the defender of darkness. He is the God of Night, Darkness and Dreams. It is only his constant vigil of darkness that protects us from the demons of Va'Decheiu and Va'Nhegel. His image is humanoid, gaunt and focused.

Va'Gharana, The goddess of the arts and seduction, playful and beautiful; she coaxes the artistic side of each being. With the artistic side comes the passionate, so she is also regarded as the seductress.

Humans

Emperor Jayess, Emperor from 3883 – 3955. He commanded the rewriting of the Book of Illust Creation. His version was studied and used in the Human Empire for many millennia

Emperor Ramerko, Emperor from 6992 to 7045. He delivered the Emperor Jayess version of the Book of Illust Creation to the Elves in 7030.

Vicar Prinot, a priest of Va'Haluc

Terrali:

Graycliand. Though not a majority of Terrali venture away from their forest, many do. The Terrali still fear the fate of Emminda so they are very careful when they travel to trade or study. Graycliand, like most Terrali, dyed her hair brown. Blonde hair is only a Human, Dwarf or Giantfolk gene on Budora. An Elf with blonde hair would be considered tainted and suspect. Terrali are careful to blend in with the Elves.

Kybrand. The unlucky Terrali sent to find herbs in the meadow who discovered Graycliand's case.

Niot.. The half-blind herbalist of Tarbenlief.

Montrealu. The Tarbenlief Elder who studied Tirweul magic.

Bleithz, Chantrietta, Aewanne, Kelfaine, and Jennser and hundreds more. The Nighthunters.

Nhegelians

Clewenid A Tireweul Elf, vessel of the Nhegelian channel

Raenick A Tireweul Elf, vessel of the Nhegelian channel, possessor of Graycliand, and discoverer of Haluc's bane.

Other Elves

Karoutes-ven, High Elven Priestess. She accepted the Book of Illust Creation in 7030 from Emperor Ramerko ending three millennia of bad relations between Elves and Humans.

Wittig-ven, devout priest of Va'Haluc, mentor of Vicar Printot He was raised and trained in Tesvo-nar, the largest Elven City-State. He is half-elven.

Ubjean, a young Elven priest and friend of Wittig.

Dietrel, the chatty innkeeper in Floarta, a suburban village of Tesvo-nar.

Dwarves

The bickering couple who owned the bar outside Merratte-nar, not far from their dwarven home town in the Rodalspine mountains.

The Tale of the Terrali Nighthunters

Atvia

De'Heatah, nursemaid to Va'Treala and protector of the Black Forest. It is unknown how many of her kind are left on Budora. They are said to live in tiny villages built on the highest mountaintops.

Goblins

Goharo, the cranky goblin who helps De'Heatah guard the Black Forest from visitors in exchange for solice.

Appendix II: Budora

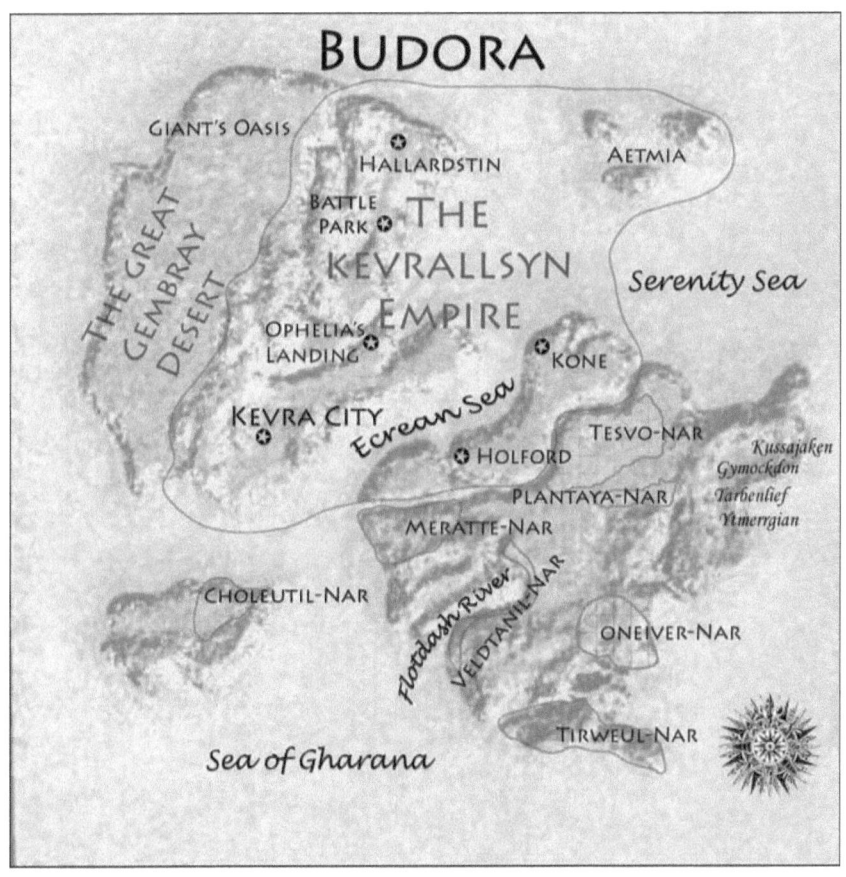

www.ingramcontent.com/pod-product-compliance
Lightning Source LLC
Chambersburg PA
CBHW031605260626
47154CB00020B/1580

* 9 7 8 0 6 1 5 1 8 2 6 1 2 *